THE *RIVER* IS *HOME*

THE RIVER IS HOME

A NOVEL

PATRICK D. SMITH

FOREWORD BY PATRICK D. SMITH JR.

PINEAPPLE PRESS
Palm Beach, Florida

Pineapple Press
An imprint of The Rowman & Littlefield Publishing Group, Inc.
4501 Forbes Boulevard, Suite 200, Lanham, Maryland 20706
www.rowman.com

Distributed by NATIONAL BOOK NETWORK

British Library Cataloguing in Publication Information Available

Library of Congress Cataloging-in-Publication Data

Smith, Patrick D., 1927–2014
The river is home / Patrick D. Smith.
p. cm.
1. River life—Fiction. I. Title.
PS3569.M53785R58 2012
813'.54—dc23
2012026338

ISBN 9781683342847 (pbk. : alk. paper) | ISBN 9781683342854 (epub)

♾™ The paper used in this publication meets the minimum requirements of American National Standard for Information Sciences—Permanence of Paper for Printed Library Materials, ANSI/NISO Z39.48-1992.

FOREWORD

ONE DAY in early 1951 my father, who was twenty-one at the time, rolled a sheet of paper into his typewriter and started writing "A gentle breeze was blowing through the cypress trees as Abner Corey sat on the stoop of his shack mending fish traps." He finished one page, then set it aside. A few weeks later he looked at that sheet and decided he wanted to find out if he could write a novel. Ten days later, *The River Is Home* was finished.

He showed it to his professor and friend at Ole Miss, who surprised him by telling him he needed to get it published. Not knowing how to do that and having the boldness of youth, he researched publishers and chose Little, Brown and Co. thinking it was a small operation and more likely to take a chance on a first novel. He then packaged up his manuscript and sent it along with a note, "My name is Patrick Smith and this is my novel, *The River Is Home*. Please publish it immediately."

Lo and behold, they did just that. He became the youngest published author in Mississippi at that time.

He chose as his locale for his coming-of-age story the lower Pearl River in Mississippi. It is set at the beginning of the eighteenth century and the dialog is written in the vernacular of that time and place. It revolves around thirteen-year-old Skeeter Corey, who knows and loves the swamp. He can skin a deer, row a skiff upstream, and pop the head off a snake with his bare hands. He can throw his knife and split a playing card from 100 feet, a skill he never intended to use on a man.

The Coreys are good people, though illiterate due to lack of opportunity. Growing weary of life as sharecroppers, they moved to the swamps of the river where they eke out a meager living by fishing and selling their catch to the townspeople, who disparagingly call them "river rats" yet enjoy the fruits of their dangerous labor. It's a hard yet happy life on the river but outside forces seem determined to collide with their way of life. The result leads to tragedy and a reckoning for Skeeter.

You only have to read the first few pages to see why that professor encouraged dad, feeling that people would be drawn to this story set on the banks of a southern river. Through his words, he takes you to that time and place. Each character is so well developed that you feel you have met them somewhere, sometime.

Through his descriptions of the plants, weather, smells, and moods of the river, you will be there, swatting away "skeeters," watching the shadows play under a big cypress tree as the murky water laps against your canoe, nervously watching for "'gators," all the while inhaling the sweet yet fetid smell of the swamp around you. I found them so vivid that I asked him once how he knew all of that. He said that he just observed and remembered what he saw as a boy, camping and playing along the Strong River, which runs through his tiny hometown of D'Lo, Mississippi.

He wrote this before I was born. I remember reading *The River Is Home* when I was about eight years old and being impressed not only with the story but also proud that my dad was the author. It still impresses me to this day. I invite you to join the Corey family in a world not so long ago or far away.

Patrick D. Smith, Jr.
Fall 2020

THE RIVER IS HOME

ONE

A GENTLE BREEZE was blowing through the cypress trees, as Abner Corey sat on the stoop of his shack, mending fish traps. There had been a light rain that morning, and now the sun was sending long shafts of light into the swamp to draw the water up again. The drops of rain, clinging to the cypress boughs, glittered like thousands of diamonds in the air. The cries of wood ducks and cranes mingled with the chatter of squirrels and the incessant bellowing of frogs for more rain. Everything was full of activity but the Corey family. Abner's wife, Glesa, was stretched out on the back stoop basking in the sun. The two boys, Jeff and Skeeter, were throwing knives into the bare plank floor, while Theresa, the only daughter, was helping Abner mend the fish traps. The traps were the most valuable possessions of the Coreys because they represented their only means of getting cash money.

The Coreys had been living in the swamp for five years now. They had previously been sharecroppers, wandering to and from different parts of Mississippi and Louisiana year after year, getting what jobs they could and eating when they

could, but always being without much of either. And then
Abner had brought them to the Pearl River swamps of lower
Mississippi to begin a new and strange life. They arrived
with nothing and had to build their small shack with their
bare hands. Abner had chosen a little clearing on a bayou
several hundred yards from the muddy Pearl. The clearing
was bounded by tall, moss-covered, cypress trees, mingled
with magnolia and willow. From their clearing to the river
lay long stretches of flat marsh grass, and behind the clearing was the almost impenetrable swamp. The swamp was
joined by long, rolling hills covered with pine and scrub oak,
but the only way to cross from the clearing to the hills was
by boat through the murky swamp. Five miles down the river
was a little settlement called Mill Town, and twenty miles to
the north was Fort Henry. Once a week Abner and the boys
would row to Mill Town and trade fish for money and supplies, and once a year they would go to Fort Henry to sell
their winter trappings of hides. Fort Henry was a bustling
port town on the steamboat route to Jackson, far to the
north. Abner had promised the family if they ever got
enough money he would take them on the steamboat to
Jackson, but that time never seemed to come.

Most of the Coreys' time was spent on the river and in
the swamp—Abner and the boys fishing, hunting, and trap-
ping, while Glesa and the girl did the house chores and
tended the small garden on the edge of the clearing. They
grew a few onions, peas, and peppers, but their main diet
usually consisted of fish, game, and the wild poke salat that
grew along the clearing. They were planning this year to
have pork, because Abner had traded for three hogs in Mill
Town and had built a pen on the banks of the bayou.

The Corey shack was built of drift lumber and cypress
logs. The house had three rooms and no windows, and the
roof was made of hand-hewn cypress shingles stuffed with
moss. Two rooms of the house were used for sleeping, and

the other for cooking and eating. There were two beds in one room and one in the other. The beds were made of cypress slats, and the mattresses were made of croaker sacks sewn together and stuffed with moss. Ma and Pa Corey slept in one room and the boys and Theresa in the other. The kitchen contained a bare plank table, a washstand, and a clay hearth in one corner for cooking. All the water for cooking and drinking came from the bayou. The Coreys used the banks of the bayou for their privy and bath.

The oldest of the children was Jeff, who was nineteen. Theresa was fifteen and Skeeter thirteen. The Coreys had named their youngest boy Skeeter because he was born prematurely, and Pa Corey said that he was no bigger than a good-sized mosquito. Even now he was small and runty for his age, and did not have all that he should have had in the way of book-learning. Jeff was tall and skinny with short-cut, blond hair. Theresa was the most unusual of the Corey children. She was like a rose growing in a field of cabbage. She was an unusually beautiful girl with long, flaming-red hair, brown eyes, and a complexion as white as snow. It was strange that such a child could have the same blood as the haggard pair that had borne her. Ma Corey was a fat, sloppy-looking woman with straggly gray hair. Her teeth were stained brown from the long years of snuff dipping, and her skin was wrinkled and tanned from the long hours of working the fields before they came to the swamp to live. Pa Corey was built much the same as Jeff, tall and skinny, with short-cropped gray hair. Ma had always said that he could make more money hiring out as a scarecrow than he could any other way.

Pa Corey would not go into the swamp with Jeff and Skeeter to set and run their animal traps. He was more afraid of snakes and alligators than he was of the devil himself. In the spring and summer, Jeff and Skeeter would go into the swamp to kill snakes and catch young 'gators, so they could sell the snakeskins and young 'gators in Mill town. In the winter they would trap for mink and otter. Pa Corey was a fearless man on the river and bayou, but nothing could induce him into the swamp. The boys had built a flat-bottomed skiff to use in the swamp and a rowboat for the river.

As Pa Corey sat mending the traps, he often talked to himself, as he was doing now. "Dern gars," he said, "don't make nothin' but trouble fer me. Wish the slimy devils would stay out'n my nets and traps! Jest like hangin' a bull 'gator by the tail. I wish the good Lord would have a big fish fry in Heaven and use all the gars they is in the river. Pesky devils."

"Pa," said Theresa, "why is it that the gars won't stay in the traps like the catfish and the buffalo do?"

"Well, hit seems that the Lord equipped the muddy bastards with saws on their heads jest so'es they could saw their way out of anything. I've heard they can cut clear through a cypress log, jest as easy as nothin'. I caught one on a trotline once, and even the niggers wouldn't et him. They said he were a brother to the devil, and if'n you et him you would shore go below onced you was dead."

"Pa, Skeeter told me onced that he saw the devil up in the swamp one time. He said hit were jest afore dark and he come through a gap in the saw vines and there the devil set chewin' on a big ole water moccasin. He said when the devil seed him there, he swollered the snake whole and run off through the swamp belchin' smoke and bellowin' like a bull. Do you reckon hit were so, Pa?"

"Now don't you pay no mind to what Skeeter says, you hear? He's lible to come home one day sayin' he seed two bull 'gators doin' a dance in the top of a cypress tree."

"Jest the same, Pa," Theresa said, "hit shore would scare me if'n I was to see somethin' like that. That dern Skeeter jest ain't skerred of nothin', and I onced seen him ketch a live snake with his hands and pop its head clear off its body. Whut makes you so skeered of snakes, Pa?"

"Now you shet up and go tell them two boys to come here and help me git these traps in the boat. If'n we don't get 'em out soon, hit's goin' to be too dark. And I jest got a feelin' that them big ole catfish is goin' to be on a party tonight."

Theresa jumped up and ran to the room where Jeff and Skeeter were throwing the knives and said: "Pa said fer you two to git them traps in the boat so'es you can git 'em out afore it gits dark. You know Pa don't like to be on the river at night with them steamboat fellers runnin' over everything that gits in the way."

"Who's afraid of 'em?" Jeff said. "Skeeter, throw yore knife through her big ole toes."

Skeeter rose, drew back the blade, and before Theresa could run, the knife went slicing through the air and buried itself in the floor between her toes. "Oh my gosh, Pa," wailed Theresa, "Skeeter is in here tryin' to split my feet in half with his knife."

The boys jumped up and followed Theresa to the porch where Pa was sitting. Jeff said, "Dern fool! You ain't got no cause to go around the house bellowin' like that. I've seed Skeeter shave the whiskers off a tick's face at ten feet with that knife. You know dern well he don't never miss whut he aims at."

"Yeh, but they're always a fust time for everthing," said Theresa. "So jest you don't be doin' that no more."

"You dad-burned kids would make a hog's jaw bust carryin' on the way you do," said Pa. "Now git them traps on out there in the boat and let's git goin'. Theresa, you tell yore Ma to git up off that floor and hoe the garden like I tole her to. And you better help her, too."

*   *   *

Pa and the boys loaded the traps in the boat and shoved off down the bayou toward the river. They had about two miles to row before they got to the place where they were to set the traps. They did not put them in the river where it was deep but set them in little coves and branches running into the river. They set their trotline in the river and ran it along logs or sunk it deep into the water by putting heavy iron weights on the line. Pa was in the rear of the boat, and the boys sat in the middle and rowed.

They passed through the area of flat marsh grass and into the dense vegetation of the river bank. The entrance of the bayou into the river was so thick with cypress and magnolias that a person not familiar with it could pass right by, without knowing it. Pa said that was a good thing because it would keep the river folks and the sporting men from Fort Henry from messing around their place. The water, where the bayou met the river, looked like a pot of boiling mud. The Coreys could never remember the river when it wasn't muddy, but the bayou was always clear. Pa believed the big gar fighting on the river bottom kept the mud stirred up all the time.

When they reached the river, Jeff and Skeeter had to put all the strength they had into rowing the boat upstream. The river was always swift; even in the summer when there was not much rain and the water was low, it was full of trick currents and whirlpools. They had once seen a big log go down in the middle of the river and shoot high into the air a hundred yards from where it went under. Sometimes the channel would change overnight, and the steamboats would run aground and have to be pulled out of the mud.

About a mile above the Corey bayou, the river made a big turn and cut to the west for a few miles. This was known as West Cut. Along the turn there were several coves and creeks running into the river. When they reached the turn, they cut into an almost hidden cove along the west bank.

This cove was Pa Corey's favorite place for placing his fish traps. The big cats and buffalo would come into the cove at night to feed on the smaller fish and swim into his cone-shaped traps. He had caught as much as two hundred pounds of fish in one night here.

After they had carefully laid the traps and tied the trap lines to stobs, they cut back into the river to see about their trotline. When they came to the line, the boys headed the boat downstream so Pa could work it from the back of the boat. The hooks were baited with big chunks of squirrel and rabbit meat, and Pa had several piles of the cut meat in the boat to bait the hooks that were empty. About halfway down the line he jumped up and started shouting wildly: "Gol dern sons of bitches! Why can't the dirty devils let a feller make a livin' in peace?"

"Whut's the matter, Pa?" asked Jeff.

"Matter!" cried Pa. "Look at this! A dern catfish head without no body. That cat woulda weighed at least twenty pounds. Hit's the dad-nabbed turtles did it. If'n it ain't them thievin' devils, hit's the blame gar tearin' up the traps and nets. They ought to be some way to outdo these critters."

"I knows a old nigger down at Mill Town that could fix it so the gar and turtle wouldn't mess around with no fish lines," said Skeeter. "He done learned to mix up some potion you kin rub on the lines that makes them critters turn their tails and run. Let's see whut he kin do next week, Pa."

"We'll shore have to do somethin', Skeeter," said Pa, "or hit won't be wuth while to even fish in this muddy ole river."

"Pa," said Jeff, "hit's goin' to be dark pretty soon and it's jest about time fer that steamboat to come round the bend. You better hurry up or we all lible to be swimmin' home stead of ridin' in this here boat."

"You mighty right," said Skeeter. "You shore better git done with them lines, Pa, afore that steamboat feller gits here."

Pa Corey finished baiting the last hook, and they turned the bow of the boat downstream towards home. The last rays of light were fading through the tall cypress trees, when they reached the mouth of the bayou that led to their home. About halfway through the marsh flats, they heard a loud blast and saw fire and smoke belch above the treetops.

"Jest listen to that feller sound off," said Pa. "You would think the idiot owns the river the way he tries to blow the tops off all the trees."

The steamboat men did not like the people who lived along the banks of the river and in the swamps. They felt that the families, like the Coreys, who made their living along the river were always getting in their way and slowing down their speed. Sometimes the boatmen would purposely go close to the bank and run through trotlines just to get rid of them, and when they caught the swampmen on the river with their small boats, they would try to sink them with their wake. Once, below Mill Town, a swampman had shot a deck hand on a boat when they passed and tried to sink him, and the people in Mill Town had lynched the man without giving him a trial. The townspeople and the men on the river boats called the Coreys and their kind swamp rats, and said they were no better than the vultures living along the river banks. There was no law to protect the swamp rats, so they preferred to stay to themselves and avoid trouble as much as possible.

By the time the Coreys had put the few cats they had caught into the fish box and secured it in the bayou, Ma Corey was calling them to supper. Jeff took a bucket from the rear of the house, went to the bayou to bring in water for washing the dishes, and Pa and Skeeter went in search of wood, to keep the fire going through the night. The fire at night was their only protection against the mosquitoes, which were especially bad in the spring of the year. It was dark by the time all three got back to the house, and, as they climbed the steep steps to the kitchen, they could smell the aroma of frying fish and boiling coffee. Theresa was setting the table with their only setting of tin dishes, and Ma was bending over the mud hearth getting the pan ready to fry the corn pone. The Coreys in the last five years had eaten tons of fried fish and corn pone, which was their regular supper most every night.

"Gol dern it, Ma," Pa said, "I shore wish we hadn't had to build this blame shack so high off the ground. Hit nearly breaks my pore tired bones to climb the steps ever day."

"You jest better thank the good Lord that we did build the shack high off the ground stead of fussin' about it," said Ma. "You know dern well what will happen when the rains come and that muddy ole river comes messin' aroun' tryin' to git in the house with us."

"I reckon you right, Ma, but it shore do tire a pore ole fool like me climbin' them steps all the time."

Pa and the boys took the bar of yellow soap off the cabinet top and began washing the river slime from their hands before supper. Each took his turn at the one cloth towel that hung on a nail over the washstand. When they had finished, they sat at the table, and Theresa poured hot coffee into the tin cups before them.

"They ain't no more sugar for the coffee, Pa," said Theresa. "You better git some the next time you is in Mill Town."

"Yah," said Ma, "and if'n you don't git some more corn meal, they ain't gonna be no more pone on the table afore long. If'n you two boys would stay out'n that swamp long enough to clear me a little patch of land, I could grow us some corn to eat and to feed them pore old hogs. Them hogs air gittin' so thin hit's a wonder the snakes ain't done et 'em afore now."

"Now, they ain't no use to worry none," said Pa. "Me and the boys air goin' into town Satterday and we'll git some sugar and meal if'n them dern turtles and gar will jest leave us be long enough to haul in a mess of fish."

"You goin' to take me to town this time, Pa?" asked Theresa. "You been promisin' to take me for quite a spell now. Please take me this time, Pa."

"Now, you know why I ain't took you to town, Theresa," he said. "I done tole you a thousand times that if'n them dern town boys was to ever see you, they'd come sniffin' aroun' here and jest cause us a heap of trouble."

"Well, that ain't no reason why you can't ever take *me*," said Ma. "You know dern well ain't even no old hound dog gonna come sniffin' aroun' after me."

Ma Corey finished the frying of the bread, dumped it onto a plate and set it, with the fish, on the table. They all gathered at the table, and Skeeter slapped a fork into a big piece of the fried catfish.

"Now, jest a minute, Skeeter," said Pa. "I think I better turn up some thanks tonight afore we eat this meal." Pa turned his head towards the roof, and the others bent their heads.

"Good Lord," he said, "thank ye fer this meal. And please, Lord, keep them dern turtles and gar away from the lines afore Satterday so'es we can have some more pone on the table next week. Thank ye. Amen."

"Damn critters," he murmured to himself, as he carved a big piece from the pone before him.

"Pa," said Jeff, "me and Skeeter was thinkin' 'bout goin' into the swamp tonight after we eat and giggin' us some frogs. I heered one bellowin' last night what sounded like he was as big as a bear. Shore would be good to have some frog legs to eat in the mornin'."

"You boys had orter stay out'n that swamp in the night-time. You know the good Lord didn't make that place fer us human bein's to go into. One of these nights you goin' to go into that place and ain't gonna come out at all."

"They ain't nothin' in there that could hurt a feller if'n he jest keeps his eyes open and don't act a fool," said Jeff. "Anyhows, we ain't skeered of hit like you air."

When they finished the meal, Theresa put the dishes on the stand and began heating some water to clean the grease left on them by the fish. Ma put a big dip of snuff in her bottom lip and got the sage-straw broom to sweep the floor. Pa ambled out to the front porch to sit and think about ways to get more traps set, and Jeff and Skeeter got out their frog gigs to sharpen the points on the old whetrock that the family had had for as long as they could remember.

"Jeff," said Skeeter, "if'n we see a big moccasin in the swamp tonight, I'll show you how to ketch the varment. Maybe we kin swap him fer some likker sticks when we go to town Satterday."

"You better quit messin' with them snakes so much without any help," said Jeff. "One of them varments is goin' to knock a hole clear through you one of these days."

"Shucks," said Skeeter, "you know I ain't skeered of them snakes. I was in the swamp one day by myself and I seed a big otter stalkin' one of them buggers. I sot real still in the skiff and watched what was goin' to happen. That dern otter snuck up to that snake backwards and waved his tail at him. When the ole snake struck at that bugger's tail, that otter turned so quick and sunk his teeth behin' that snake's head I hardly saw it happen. I asked the ole otter to tell me how he done it, and that sapsucker showed me all about it. I'll show you how hit's done fust time I gits a chance."

"One of these days you goin' to turn into a gar fer tellin' them big tales like you do," said Jeff. "Sometimes you scare me when you start talkin' like what you do."

"I ain't tellin' no tale, honest, Jeff," said Skeeter. "You kin see sights sech as I do if'n you jest goes about hit in the right way."

"If'n I ever see some of the buggers you do while I'm in that swamp alone, they ain't even goin' to be no swamp left where I come tearin' my way out of there. Now, you better shet up sech talk and go git us a good lidard knot so'es we kin git goin'.'"

Skeeter took a burning stick from the hearth and went to the back of the clearing where they stacked the wood to get a fat pine knot to use as a torch. When he got back, he was slapping his neck and howling with pain. "We better git some of that oil I got and rub on us afore we leave," he said. "Them skeeters is shore out to kill a feller tonight. Dern if'n I couldn't feel the blood runnin' out'n me when that devil sucked."

"I don't know which would be the wust," said Jeff, "havin' them skeeters suck the hide off'n me or have that stinkin' crap you made smeared all over me. Hits like choosin' betwix a turtle and a gar. What you put in that stuff, anyway, Skeeter?"

"Hit's a potion a ole nigger give me at Mill Town onced. Hit's got jest about everthing in it."

"Well, I don't doubt that a bit. Now go get the stuff and let's git on in the swamp."

Skeeter went into the room where he and Jeff slept and pulled a long box from under the bed. The box contained many odds and ends and several bottles of potions that Skeeter had made for different purposes. He selected a bottle with a murky red fluid in it and went back to the kitchen where Jeff waited by the fire. When he opened the bottle, Ma dropped the broom and ran from the kitchen.

"Good gosh a mighty, Skeeter," Theresa shouted, "whut in the world is hit you got in that bottle? Hit smells like the devil's breath itself."

"Damn, Skeeter," said Jeff. "If'n hit's all the same to you, I'll jest stick by the skeeters and let you keep that stinkin' stuff to yoreself."

Ma Corey came running back to the kitchen, dragging Pa with her. "Jest git you a whif uv that stuff," she said, "and you won't worry bout eatin' no food no more. Now, you tell that dern youngin' to git that stuff out'n my kitchen and don't never bring nothin' like that in here no more. I'd jest as soon sleep with a bed uv skunks."

"Yore Ma's right, Skeeter," he said. "You'll have all the buzzards comin' from the swamp to see what's dead in the house."

"Derned if'n I'm goin' to have the skeeters eatin' on me, even if'n I do have to smell like a barrel of skunk juice," said Skeeter.

Jeff lit the pine knot, and they went into the yard. Skeeter stopped and rubbed the mosquito potion on his face and arms, and they loaded the gigs and poles into the light skiff and shoved off up the bayou.

"Who's goin' to pole, and who's goin' to gig tonight, Jeff?" asked Skeeter. "If'n I'm goin' to pole, you better git up here and hold this lidard knot afore we gits into that thick brush."

"You mout as well stay up there and do the giggin' whilst you're there," said Jeff, "cause you're a sight better shot with that thing than I am."

"Well, ifn't I'm goin' to stay up here, you be shore and go slow, so if'n I see me a snake I kin ketch him."

"I'll be derned if'n you do," said Jeff. "If'n you start draggin' live snakes in this here boat with me in here where I can't see good, I'm lible to pull down yore pants and spank yore rear plenty good."

A few hundred yards from the house the straight banks of the bayou melted into a seemingly unending lake of water and trees. This was the beginning of the great swamp. The water was shallower and darker, and the trees and vines looked almost impenetrable from a distance. It would be suicide for anyone not familiar with the swamp to venture into the place at night; even Jeff and Skeeter would not go in then, but they had made many trips around the edges in search of frogs. Danger dwelled in every tree and vine, and at any minute swift death could strike out of a dark shadow. The low-hanging branches and vines were covered with water moccasins, which had crawled there in search of safety from the alligators that lurked around the logs and shallow places. The alligators would conceal themselves during the day and come out at night for food. Deeper in the swamp there were even more dangerous enemies—panther and wild cat, and they had been known to attack a man by day or night. The water itself smelled of death and decay.

"Jeff," said Skeeter, "let's go over to that mudbank close to that old fallen magnolia tree. I seed sign there the other day where them big ole bull frogs had been sittin' on their haunches and rubbin' each other."

"O.K.," said Jeff, "but you hold that light good and high so'es I kin see some. Hit's so dark in here tonight that you could see a nigger's eye ten miles off. And I derned shore don't want to git this skiff stuck and have to pull it out."

"Pole her a little mite to the left, Jeff," said Skeeter. "They's two eyes over there as big as saucers starin' at me."

Jeff poled the skiff gently to the left, while Skeeter stood in the bow with the torch in his left hand and the gig in his right.

"Lordy me, Jeff," said Skeeter, "look at the size of that feller. I'd bet that bugger would weigh five pounds. I'd hate to see that sucker jump as high as he could. He'd probably land down at Mill Town."

"Well, quit runnin' yore mouth so loud and drop that gig betwix his eyes afore he leaps in the water and makes some big 'gator a good supper."

Jeff stopped the skiff and dug his pole deep into the muck to hold it steady. Skeeter raised the gig high above his head, took a steady aim, and sailed it towards the white eyes of the frog. The gig struck the bank with a thud and dropped into the water.

"Did you git him, Skeeter?" asked Jeff.

"I ain't sure. I didn't see him jump when the gig struck, but the gig didn't stick to the bank. Pole her up and let me git the gig out'n the water."

Jeff drew the pole out of the soft muck and shoved the skiff further towards the bank. "Hold her there," said Skeeter. "I think I kin reach hit from here."

Skeeter bent down in the skiff and reached into the black water for the long handle of the gig. When he raised it from the water, one end had sunk so he knew that his aim had been true.

"My gosh, Jeff," he said, as he pulled the gig back into the skiff. "Look at them legs. Bet they air at least two feet long."

"One more like that will be all we kin eat fer breakfast," said Jeff. "Let's find one more so'es we kin git the heck out'n here."

Jeff poled the skiff further along the edges of the swamp, while Skeeter held the torch high in search of more eyes. At times Skeeter had to lie flat in the skiff to pass under the low-hanging buck vines. They pushed farther and farther into the swamp.

"Hold her, Jeff," said Skeeter, "I think I seed some eyes a little over to the right uv you. Push her over there and let's see what hit is."

Jeff swung the skiff further to the right until the owner of the eyes came into the range of the light. "Hit shore air another big frog," said Skeeter. "He looks like he mout be as big as the other one. Pole her in and let me git a throw."

Jeff dug the pole into the muck, and Skeeter again took aim with his right hand, while holding the torch with his left. He raised the gig high, and it hit the bank with a dull thud. Only this time the gig pinned the frog to the bank.

"I shore got me a perfect hit that time," said Skeeter. "Pole her up and let me git the bugger in the skiff."

Jeff poled the skiff close to the bank, and Skeeter put the frog in the bottom of the skiff with the other one. "How's you and the skeeters gittin' along, Jeff?" he asked. "Bet them buggers has sucked you dry by now, ain't they?"

"Yeh, but I'd still ruther they kilt me than to die of that awful stuff you put on you. Now let's git back to the house afore that lidard knot has done burned out and we air left in a mess."

Skeeter laid the gigs flat in the bottom of the skiff and crouched in the bow to hold the torch so Jeff could see. They were slowly making their way back through the vines towards the bayou, when Skeeter saw the biggest pair of eyes he had ever seen in the swamp at night.

"Look over there, Jeff," he said. "Do you see them lights what I see? Them looks like the runnin' lights on the back end uv a steamboat. Let's go see if'n one of them blame boats has done run into the swamp."

Jeff poled the skiff closer so that Skeeter could get a better look at the enormous eyes which had caught the glare of the torch. As they got nearer, the eyes grew larger and larger. "Hit must be the reflection of the moon on the water, only they ain't no moon out tonight," said Skeeter. "And look, Jeff, they air turnin' as red as a tomato."

"Them shore ain't the eyes of no frog," said Jeff, "so'es you better be careful up there in the front of this thing."

After they had moved a few more feet forward, Skeeter signaled Jeff to stop. He stood up and held the torch higher so he could get a better look. "Pole her back a mite," he said. "They's a bull 'gator lyin' there that must be a grand-daddy to all the 'gators in the swamp. I'll bet his hide would be wuth more'n all the snakeskins in the swamp."

"Yeh, but don't go gittin' no funny idea 'bout me and you tryin' to git that hide. I'd jest as soon that critter keep his hide and me keep mine. I'm goin' to pole this skiff out'n here and leave well enough be."

"Jest a minute, Jeff, don't go fer a little yet. I got a idea where we mout be able to take this critter home with us tonight. If'n I could jest sink this gig deep enough betwix his eyes, we could let him flounce till he's dead and then drag him in. He's bound to be wuth enough to keep us in sugar and meal fer a month."

"I'd druther do without no corn pone and drink my coffee straight than wrestle with that big devil. So'es you jest forget them ideas and let's git out'n here."

Jeff pulled the pole from the muck and started to back the skiff out, and Skeeter realized what he was doing. Skeeter was not willing to leave the prize without even a try, so when Jeff started backing the skiff away, he lifted the gig and let it fly with all the strength his body could give forth, straight at the red eyes of the bull alligator. The shaft sailed true and struck the alligator between the eyes with a sickening thud. When the gig struck, the 'gator bellowed with such force that it nearly knocked Skeeter from the bow of the skiff.

"I got him, Jeff, I got him," cried Skeeter. "Pole up a little closer so'es I can see if'n he's dead."

Jeff poled up close to the burning eyes, and the 'gator did not move. The gig was planted solidly between its eyes. When he got a little closer, Skeeter signaled for him to stop and said, "He shore am dead, Jeff. I'll grab hold of the gig shaft and you back off till we git him to floatin'. Then we'll work him to the back, and you kin hold the shaft while I kin pole from up here. We kin drag him in home, and won't Ma be proud when she sees this?"

Skeeter grabbed the shaft, while Jeff poled the skiff back into deeper water. Suddenly the entire swamp seemed to turn over and cry to heaven. The skiff went round and round with Skeeter holding his grip on the gig shaft. Jeff was thrown to the bottom of the skiff.

"Turn loose that thing, Skeeter," cried Jeff, "'fore that critter turns us over and kills the both of us!"

Before Skeeter could turn loose the shaft, he was slung through the air and thrown bodily into a group of cypress knees. The torch hit the water and went out in a sizzle of smoke. Skeeter was still holding to the shaft, and he felt himself being pulled through the murky slime at a fast rate of speed. Finally, from sheer exhaustion, he relaxed his grip from the shaft, and sank slowly into the muck.

Jeff was knocked dizzy for a moment, but raised slowly to his feet. "My God, Skeeter," he cried. "Where are you?" No sound came from the darkness except the echo of his own voice. In a few moments he thought he heard a faint moan to his right. It sounded as if it was about twenty yards from the skiff.

"Skeeter," he cried aloud, "kin you hear me?" Still no answer. Oh my Lord! he thought to himself, Skeeter's done bin kilt.

But then a second moan came, and now he heard it clearly. He took the pole and edged the skiff in the direction of the sounds. The moans became louder, and he cried out again. This time Skeeter answered him in a low voice: "Jeff! Air that you? Is the frogs still in the skiff?"

"Dern fool," said Jeff, "you askin' 'bout them frogs and me worried sick that 'gator done kilt you. Where is you? You better git in here afore them snakes finish you fer sure."

"Jest hold the skiff still and keep talkin', and I'll come to you," said Skeeter.

"Well, if'n you don't git here afore long, I'm shore goin' to be shoutin' so loud them folks in the hills will hear me."

Jeff felt a pull at the side of the skiff and knew that Skeeter had reached him. "Wait jest a minute and let me git up there and help you in," he said. "We don't want to turn this thing over."

Jeff crawled to the bow of the skiff and grabbed Skeeter by the arms. He slowly pulled him forward until he felt his body roll into the bottom of the skiff. Then he inched his way back to the rear. They sat in silence for a minute, trying to get their eyes accustomed to the darkness.

"Now ain't you done got us in a hell uv a mess!" said Jeff. "How you think we is ever goin' to get home without no light? And I done tole you to let that damned 'gator alone."

"We kin git home," said Skeeter, "if'n we kin jest holler loud enough to git Pa to hear us. Then he kin holler back and we kin go to his voice."

"Yeah, and have them moccasins drappin' all over our shoulders. I'll swear, Skeeter, I shore ought to whop the stuffin' out'n you if'n we ever git out'n this."

Skeeter and Jeff stood up in the skiff and shouted as loud and as long as they could, but they received no answer.

"Hit's only about nine o'clock," said Skeeter. "If'n we jest sit still a few more minutes till the stars come out I kin shore git us home. I know one star that lies right over the house. I've laid awake plenty of nights and looked up and seed it. And onced when I were in the swamp a 'gator tole me that if'n I ever git lost at night jest to make fer that star, and I would shore git home again."

"Well, I hope to the good Lord that this air one time when yore tales makes some sense," said Jeff.

Jeff stuck his pole deep into the muck to keep the skiff from drifting, and they sat waiting for the stars to come out to show them the way home. Even after so much time had passed, their eyes still could not penetrate the dark of the swamp. They heard noises that they knew to be frogs and 'gators, and other noises that they had never heard before. Once they heard an awful scream that Jeff said was a panther, deep in the swamp. They could feel the flesh creeping along their bones as the swamp became more murky and mysterious. Finally the stars came out, and the moon broke through the seemingly impassable barrier of blackness.

"You see that big star at the end of the Big Dipper?" asked Skeeter. "Well, you jest count six stars to the left and four to the right in a straight line, and you'll come to a star that air a whole lot brighter than the ones around hit, and hit seems to turn to red and blue and green all the time. You see it now, Jeff?"

"Yeah, I sees hit. So you sit down in the middle and I'll start polin' towards it. And for God's sake, if'n I drap a snake off'n one of these vines on yore neck, don't turn the skiff over."

"You better be the one to worry about that," said Skeeter. "I wished you would drap one of them critters in here so'es I could show you how to ketch him. Then you wouldn't be afeered of him no more."

Jeff poled the skiff steadily in the direction of the star that Skeeter had pointed out to him, and before long they came out at the head of the bayou. "From now on," said Jeff, "I think I'd believe you if'n you tole me Ma was a wildcat. I shore am proud that you weren't tellin' no big tale this time."

They glided down the bayou to the landing at the clearing, and Skeeter slipped into the kitchen to get a lighted stick to clean the frog legs by, while Jeff secured the boat and put up the pole and the one gig they had left. After they had cleaned the frogs, they pulled off their overalls and slipped into bed.

Pa stirred in his bed and asked: "Air that you boys comin' in now?"

"Yeah, hits us, Pa," said Jeff.

"Well, you boys ought not be galavantin' around in the swamp havin' a good time til this time of night. Hit worries yore ma and me to know you air frolicin' round in them swamps."

"Yeah, Pa," said Jeff, and they pulled the covers over their heads and went to sleep.

TWO

WHEN THE FIRST RAYS of the sun were beginning to penetrate the darkness, the Corey household showed some signs of life. Theresa, who was always the first one up, was in the kitchen stoking up the coals with fresh sticks to get the fire started. By the time the sun had sprung to life, Ma Corey was pouring fresh water into the old coffee grounds and getting out the pans to prepare breakfast. Pa was standing on the front porch stretching his arms and yawning loudly. Jeff and Skeeter were still in bed with the covers pulled over their heads. Pa came into the room and shook them.

"You boys git on out of there so'es we kin go and run them traps afore some nigger beats us to 'em. The way the air smells this mornin' I'd near abouts bet a coon that them traps is plum full of fish. I kin smell 'em clear to the house here."

Jeff and Skeeter slowly arose from the bed, and made their way to the back of the house and the washstand. They took turns dousing cold water on their faces and rubbing the sleep from their eyes with the towel. Skeeter was a little sore from last night's ordeal in the swamps.

"For the love of God," said Ma, "you boys git back in there and put on them overhalls. Hit jest ain't decent runnin' aroun' here naked as a couple of jaybirds."

They hurriedly left the room and returned shortly, fully dressed. "I guess we jest didn't realize that we wasn't dressed, Ma," said Skeeter.

"Well, you be shore and examine yoreself afore you come runnin' aroun' here like that no more," said Ma. "Now you take this here bucket and go git me some fresh water so'es I kin boil this corn mush."

Skeeter took the bucket and started to the bayou, while Jeff went to bring in a supply of wood to be used during the morning. The fire was never allowed to go out in the Corey house. Pa went to the back stoop and brought in the frog legs that the boys had hung there after their return the night before.

"Jest look at the size of these legs, Ma," he said. "Them shore air goin' to be some good eatin' soon as you git 'em fried."

"They'll be good if'n I kin jest keep 'em in the fryin' pan long enough to git 'em cooked. You'd think that when them things hit that hot grease they was goin' to git up and walk right back into the swamp."

"Skeeter tole me onced that he had seed a snake swoller one of them small frogs," said Theresa, "and after a while that frog jumped plum back out uv that snake's belly."

"Well, when I git him in my belly, he shore ain't goin' to jump back again," said Pa, "and I tole you afore not to pay no mind to what Skeeter has done tole you."

In a few minutes Skeeter returned with the water, and Ma put the corn meal mush on to boil. When Jeff came in, they all sat down at the table and began their breakfast of mush, frog legs, and coffee. Jeff and Skeeter did not say a word about their encounter with the big bull alligator on the previous night. After the meal was finished, Theresa and Ma started their morning chores as Pa and the boys left the house and went to the boat landing.

"Hit shore air goin' to be a purty day, ain't hit Pa?" said Skeeter. "When we gits back from the fishin' this mornin', I think I'll go into the swamp and see if I kin git me some snake hides to trade whiles we're in Mill Town tomorrow."

"Tain't goin' to be no use to go into town tomorrow if'n they ain't no fish in the traps and on the lines this mornin'. We hardly got enough in the box at home to eat ourselves. But I jest got a feelin' that we shore made a good ketch last night. You boys put yore arms to them oars and let's git on up the river."

Jeff and Skeeter glided the boat down the bayou and out into the river. The water of the river was red with the reflection of the rising sun. Gray wisps of fog floated from the water and into the trees along the bank. The river was always beautiful early in the morning. The air had a sweet, clean smell about it, and even the mud seemed not so thick. White cranes with long legs and bills were standing in the shallow water along the banks pecking at minnows and small frogs. The trees were alive with birds and squirrels, all blending their voices to make a gay musical sound drift across the river. High overhead, the cawing of the crows mingled with the call of the wood ducks coming in from their roost in the marshes. All the creatures of the air seemed to be glad to be alive on this beautiful spring day.

When they reached West Cut, Jeff took in his oar and crept to the rear of the boat to help pull up the fish traps. Skeeter steered the bow into the cove by himself, then dropped the anchor over the side. It was always exciting for Skeeter to watch them pull up the traps. Pa took one stake line while Jeff took the other, and they slowly raised the first trap from the water. With one quick motion they flipped the trap into the bottom of the boat.

"Jest look at the fish in there!" cried Jeff. "Boy, ain't they some pretty ones!"

Pa was too excited to talk. He was running his hand into the trap and pulling out fish. Skeeter stood up and looked on with glee.

"How many air hit, Pa?" asked Skeeter.

"They's eight cat and two buffalo in here," cried Pa.

When Pa had removed all the fish from the trap, they tied the stake lines and threw the trap back over the side. Skeeter drew in the anchor and rowed the boat further back in the cove where the other trap was set. He dropped the anchor again and they pulled the trap into the boat.

"We didn't do as good here," said Pa, "but they's about four good-sized cats here. Now let's hurry up and git to that trotline out in the river and see about hit afore them gars gits to work on hit."

Jeff climbed back to the middle of the boat, and he and Skeeter backed the boat out of the cove and into the river. They always liked going back better than they did coming. The swift river current caught the boat and sent it sailing downstream, like a feather floating on the water. They glided out of the swift water and pointed the bow toward the log where one end of the trotline was tied. Just before the bow touched the log, Jeff pulled hard with the oar on his side, and it swung round and pumped Pa right into the beginning of the line. When Pa had the line in his hand, the boat gently swung back around and pointed the bow downstream. Then he started pulling along the line.

The first few hooks he came to were empty of bait, but he could feel a hard pulling of the line a few feet on down and knew that he had a fish. He pulled the line up slowly. It was impossible to see below the surface of the muddy water so, in order to find what was on the hook, it was necessary to pull the line all the way out of the water. Since Pa certainly did not want to jerk any gar into the boat, he was always very slow in seeing what was on the hook. When the top of the line came out of the water, it was covered with a white, silky slime, so he knew at once without raising it any further.

"One of you boys mout as well hand me yore knife," said Pa, "they's a fish eel on this 'un, and I could shore never git him off."

Skeeter handed him his knife, and he wrapped the line around his hand several times and cut it from the trotline. Then he pulled the eel into the bottom of the boat. It was about five feet long and bigger around than Pa Corey's arm. "Hit's shore a nice 'un," said Pa, "and hit weighs 'bout six pounds."

"That's the best eatin' they air in the river," said Skeeter. "I'd heap ruther have hit than cat or buffalo."

"You mighty right," said Jeff. "I don't believe I ever could git me a bellyful of that fish eel meat."

Pa pulled the boat slowly on along the line and took off two more small catfish. At the far end he thought it had hung on a snag, so he asked Jeff to help him pull it loose. Jeff crept to the back of the boat, and they both took the line and pulled. All at once it snapped from their hands and disappeared beneath the water. "Well, I'm damned!" said Pa. "We shore got us somethin' here. Hand me the gaff Skeeter."

He took the gaff from Skeeter, and he pushed the hook deep under the water to catch and bring the line back up. When he had it again, he and Jeff grabbed the line with both hands and pulled with all the strength they could gather. They would pull up a little and then the line would go back down. They battled back and forth for a half hour and finally succeeded in getting the fish's head to the surface of the water. Pa grabbed the gaff and sliced the point through the bottom jaw of the fish. They let the line go and both took the handle of the gaff. With a mighty heave they pulled in the fish. It stretched half the length of the boat. The big cat would weigh at least eighty pounds.

"We shore got us one this time, ain't we Pa!" said Jeff.

"I knowed whut hit was goin' to be this mornin'," said Pa, "'cause I could smell hit in the air. A feller kin jest 'bout tell whut he's got afore he leaves the house if'n he'll jest smell the air."

"If'n we would of caught one more, this boat would have shore sunk," said Skeeter. "She's jest about under the water now. How much do you suppose all this fish will weigh, Pa?"

"Best I kin figger is that they'll weigh nigh on three hundred and fifty pounds with whut we got at the house. And they was bringing five cents a pound last week in Mill Town. We'll have enough left over after gittin' the supplies to buy us a few more shot and some powder fer the gun. We's jest about out."

On the way back downstream, Jeff and Skeeter didn't use the oars for fear of tipping the boat too much and swamping it. The sides were only a couple of inches out of the water, and a slight dip to one side would have sent it under. They let the current take the boat, and Jeff used his oar for a rudder. About a half mile from the mouth of the bayou they heard a loud blast around the bend.

"Oh my Lord, have mercy on me!" cried Pa. "Hit's one of them steamboat fellers, and with this load on here they will swamp us shore."

"Do you reckon we kin make hit to the bayou afore they gits to us, Pa?" asked Skeeter.

"We'd nary make it, Son," said Pa. "If'n you and Jeff was to use the oars fer speed you'd turn the boat over afore we got near 'bouts there."

The blast sounded again, and then they could see the steamboat come around the bend and head straight for them.

"Head her into that little creek comin' in there!" cried Pa.

Jeff turned the oar hard to the left, and the boat began to swing slowly into the right bank of the river. A little creek flowed into the river just below them, and Jeff pointed the bow of the boat into it. All three jumped out into the neck-deep water, and guided the boat behind a clump of bushes hanging over the water. Skeeter could hardly keep his nose above the water by standing on his toes. Just as they got behind the bush the steamboat passed, with its stern wheels churning madly. The waves from its wake rolled into the creek and knocked Skeeter from his feet. Jeff and Pa clung to the sides of the boat to keep the water from rushing over it and turning it over. Skeeter was knocked under the boat and then into the bank. When he came up, his eyes and mouth were filled with the foul-tasting, muddy water. He pulled himself onto the bank and began to belch the water from his stomach. Pa and Jeff still clung to the sides of the boat, with the waves rushing over their heads. When the water finally calmed again, they crawled onto the bank with Skeeter.

"You hurt, Skeeter?" asked Pa.

"Naw," he said, "jest got me a bellyful uv mud."

"How we goin' to git back in the boat without turnin' her over?" asked Jeff. "That sucker jest air goin' to stay out'n the water by itself now."

"I guess they ain't but one thing fer us to do," said Pa, "and that be to cling to the sides of the boat and float her in home. Me and you kin git on one side apiece and Skeeter kin hang on to the rear. We kin drift to the bayou and then kick her on up home."

Pa and Jeff got on opposite sides of the boat and Skeeter clung to the rear; they paddled with their hands and feet and pushed the boat into the swift current of the river. They fought the boat to the left side of the river and barely managed to turn it into the mouth of the bayou. Once out of the swift water, they all three clung to the rear and kicked up

their feet, and slowly moved up the bayou to the landing. Ma
and Theresa ran from the house to meet them.

"Whut in the world air you fellers hangin' on and kickin'
like a bunch of hound dogs fer?" asked Ma. "You ain't got
tetched in the head, has you?"

"That dern steamboat jest liked to have sunk the boat
and drowned us all," said Pa, "and we couldn't git back in
without swampin' her. You see whut a load we got in the
boat, don't you? We shore got to git us a bigger boat
somehow."

"Hit's a good thing you come home with some fish this
mornin'," said Ma, "or hit would have been mighty pore
eatin' aroun' here soon. Now you kin jest git me a fresh bottle of snuff fer some of that fish tomorrow."

"And if'n you kin, I'd like a hair comb, Pa," said Theresa.

"The both of you better be glad if'n I bring home plenty
of meal and sugar," said Pa, "cause we come mighty nigh
losin' the whole bunch of hit."

"Well, I'm goin' an' hoe in the garden some more," said
Ma, "so'es hit won't be too long afore we has some peas and
onions on the table. Theresa, you better go see if'n you kin
get some of that poke salat to fix fer dinner. And while you
is out there, git some fer them hogs. They been rootin' in
that pen so much hit looks like where a bunch of bull 'gators been fightin'."

Pa and the boys pulled the boat up on the landing and
took the fish out and put them in the fish box. When they
had finished, they turned the boat up on one side and
dumped the water out of it. "Jeff," said Pa, "I speck me and
you better row over to the woods on the other side of the
river and git some pine fer the fire. They ain't too much left,
and we shore won't be able to go afore next week."

"Do you want me to go too, Pa?" asked Skeeter.

"I'm afeared they won't be enough room in the boat fer
us and the wood too if'n you go," said Pa.

As soon as Jeff went to the house and brought back the ax, he and Pa shoved off down the bayou in the boat. Skeeter stood on the landing and watched them until they were out of sight. He was glad that they had not wanted him to go along with them. He liked to be alone, especially if he could go into the swamp by himself. He ran to the back of the house and got the pole for the skiff and started up the bayou toward the swamp. The sun felt good, so he pulled off his shirt and threw it in the bow. He felt good all over, knowing that he could do as he pleased the rest of the morning.

When he reached the edge of the swamp, he would give a hard push with the pole and then lie down in the bottom of the skiff and glide along, looking up into the trees and at the clouds in the sky. It gave him a dizzy feeling to lie in the skiff and watch the white clouds sail by over him. He would lie on his stomach and push the skiff along by pulling his hands through the cool water. He felt more at home in the swamp than any place he had ever been. He couldn't understand why anyone would be afraid of the swamp like Pa was.

A thought suddenly struck him that made him get to his feet and start poling the skiff swiftly through the water. He would go back to the place where they had fought the 'gator last night and see what had happened to him. He guided the skiff around trees and through vines, toward the place where they had been. Ahead of him he heard a splash in the water and knew that a snake had heard him coming and dropped from a limb or a vine. He could see turtles resting on logs and minnows shoot out in all directions. Sometimes he would pass a frog bed and see thousands of the small black eggs stretched out in long lines of white slime. As he went further into the swamp, the trees grew thicker, and the sun was almost shut out from him. He did not think that they had gone this far the night before.

Presently he came to the spot where they had first seen the burning red eyes. He found the mudbank where the 'gator had been lying and could see signs of the struggle. He poled in the direction the 'gator had pulled him, and could see broken vines for several hundred yards until he came to a limb of a tree hanging low over the water, where he found the shaft of the gig floating in the water. The 'gator must have gone under the limb and broken the shaft from the steel gig. He knew that the gig was still solidly planted in the 'gator's head. He said to himself: "Them dern 'gators must be awful hard critters to kill. Next time I go after me one of them buggers I'm shore goin' to take that shotgun with me." Without the gig shaft sticking up to break the vines, the trail was harder to follow and, when he came to a pool of deeper water, he lost it completely. He made several circles around the place, but could never pick up the trail again. Then he poled the skiff slowly in the direction of the bayou, stopping several times to watch a fight between a hawk and a catbird, or a snake stalking a small, unsuspecting frog, but he could never get close enough to one of the snakes to have a try at catching it. Sometimes it seemed that the snakes knew that he was after them and would glide away.

When he saw several small streaks of mud shoot through a shallow place by an old log, he knew that it was a crawfish bed, so he stopped the skiff and eased over the side into the water. He sunk down halfway to his knees in the soft black muck, and could feel it ooze up through his toes. He liked the feel of the cool muck on his feet. As he walked slowly through the shallow water to the log, he could see the crawfish backing around through the muck, so he stopped down and grabbed at them with his hands. When he would catch one he would put it in his pocket and then look for others. He ran his hands along the bottom of the log and caught several each time. After a while he had both of his pockets full and all he could carry in his hands, so he made his way back through the muck and dumped them into the skiff. Then he repeated this until he could find no more. He knew that his mother would be real proud, for now she could make them a big pot of crawfish gumbo. His mouth watered at the thought of this favorite dish. They could not catch crawfish in the bayou because the turtles would eat them as fast as they would come out of their beds.

It was about an hour before high noon when he reached the head of the bayou, so he lay down in the bottom of the skiff to enjoy the warm sun. A gentle breeze pushed the skiff slowly down the bayou. The breeze made the tall marsh grass look like a sea of swaying dancers. Skeeter thought that he would be content to drift forever with the sun and breeze and water about him. Why would anybody ever want to live anywhere besides along the swamp and river? When he raised up, he saw that he had already drifted past the landing, so he poled the skiff back to the landing and pulled it up on the bank.

He walked to the house and got a bucket and went back to the landing. He scooped several handfuls of the soft, cool, bayou muck into the bucket, and then put several layers of grass on top of it. When he had put in about a cupful of water and dumped the crawfish into the bucket, he walked back to the house and climbed the steps to the kitchen, where Ma and Theresa had already started preparing the noon meal.

"Guess whut I got in the bucket, Ma?" said Skeeter.

"Hit's probably a bucketful of them swamp snakes," said Theresa.

"Well if'n that's whut hit air you shore better git out'n here with hit in a hurry," said Ma. "You oughta know better than to bring a bunch of them varmints in here."

"Hain't neither one of you got the right idea," said Skeeter, "I got a plum bucketful of crawfish here that I caught in the swamp."

"Well, now, ain't that nice?" said Ma. "I'll get yore Pa to git me a few things in town tomorrow, and we'll have the best pot of gumbo you ever tasted. I'm shore right proud of you, Skeeter."

"Whut's that you got cookin' fer dinner, Ma?" he asked.

"Hit's somethin' you like a lot," said Theresa.

"We got a pot of young poke salat with little onions and peppers chopped up in hit, and I'm makin' a corn pone with onions fried in hit. And best of all, I'm fryin' that fish eel. Now ain't that a right fancy dinner, Skeeter?"

The mention of the food and the smells coming from the hearth made Skeeter's mouth water with hunger. He put the bucket of crawfish in the corner of the kitchen, and slipped up to the hearth where the eel was cooking, to steal a piece. Ma saw what he was doing and grabbed him by the arm. "Now you git on out of here and wait fer yore Pa and Jeff to git back afore you start snitchin' food. All you'll do is ruin yore dinner."

Skeeter went out the kitchen door and down to the landing. He broke sticks into little pieces and threw them into the water and imagined they were boats on a big ocean and he was sailing them. He looked down the bayou and saw Pa and Jeff coming with the load of wood. When they were close enough, he waded into the water and grabbed the bow of the boat and pulled it to the bank, as Pa and Jeff started throwing the fat pine wood out of the boat.

"You should have been with us this time, Skeeter," said Jeff. "We saw a big buck over in the woods. We had sot down on a log to rest, and we were real quiet when we heard him comin' through the bresh. He run right up to us and jest stopped and looked at us fer a spell. If'n we'd had the gun, we coulda kilt him as easy as shootin' a squirrel."

Skeeter's eyes grew wide at the mention of the deer.

"I ain't never seed as many deer signs as they were over there this mornin'," said Pa. "I guess they ain't been none of them slickers from up at Fort Henry messin' aroun' over there and skeerin' 'em fer a long time now. We'll go over there next week and git us one of them buggers."

"Kin I go too, Pa?" asked Skeeter.

"Shore you kin go. Hit's jest that when we go after wood they ain't no room to take you, and other than that we jest don't have no call to go into the woods very often."

Skeeter had never been into the big woods on the other side of the river, and the thought of getting to go made him feel wild with excitement. He could picture all kinds of mysteries that he had never seen, but he didn't think that he would like it better than the swamp.

He helped Pa and Jeff store the wood beside the house, and then they all went in to wash up for dinner. Each took his turn at the washbasin and towel. Skeeter had become so excited at the thought of the deer hunt that he forgot to tell Pa and Jeff that he had caught the crawfish.

Ma put the dinner on the table, and they sat down to begin the meal. The young poke salat, hush puppies, and eel tasted so good that they all put large quantities of the food in their mouths and ate in silence. About halfway through the meal several of the crawfish escaped from the bucket in the corner and were crawling toward the table. Pa happened to glance at the floor and saw them coming toward him. He tried to jump from his chair, but his feet caught the bottom of the table and turned him over, rolling him backwards over the floor, right into the middle of the crawfish. The half-swallowed food stuck in his throat, and he fought madly to get back to his feet. Finally he dashed to the door and looked back and saw that his assailants were only harmless crawfish.

"Where in the tarnation of hell did them things come from?" he bellowed. "I thought all the devils in the swamp were comin' after me. That liked to have scared me to death."

"Skeeter caught 'em in the swamp whiles you were gittin' the wood," said Ma. "Now come on and finish yore dinner and stop actin' like an idiot."

Everyone had to hold their breath for a minute to keep from laughing at Pa.

"Well, if'n hit weren't for the fact that I could eat six barrels of that gumbo you make, Ma, I would whale the daylights out uv Skeeter right here and now. Ain't no use in scarin' the livin' out'n a feller like that."

Skeeter got up and caught the crawfish, put them back into the bucket, got a pan and covered the top of the bucket so that they could not escape again, and the meal was finished in peace.

When the last person got up from the table, there was not a crumb of the dinner left. Theresa stacked the dishes on the stand, and she and Ma went to the other room to lie down and rest a few minutes before washing them and cleaning the kitchen. Pa and Jeff lay down on the front porch, and Skeeter went down to the bayou to lie in the grass and look up at the clouds. The sun sent pleasant waves of simmering heat into the Corey clearing, and the breeze brought cool air from the bayou. In a few minutes the entire family was fast asleep.

It was midafternoon when the blast from the steamboat whistle awakened Pa Corey from his deep sleep. He grumbled something about where he wished the steamboats would go, and rose slowly to his feet. Ma and Theresa were cleaning up the kitchen. Jeff was still asleep on the porch. Pa walked into the kitchen, took the gourd dipper from the shelf, dipped it in the bucket, and took a long draught of the cool water. He walked back to the front porch and shook Jeff. "You better git up, Son," he said. "We got to string them fish afore hit gits dark."

Pa went into the kitchen and took the long fish string from a nail on the wall. On one end of the string was a slim copper spike, and on the other a copper circle. He went down the back steps and to the landing. Skeeter was not there, and the skiff was gone. Pa found a small round stick about a foot long, pulled a loop of the line through the copper circle and pushed the stick through the loop. Then he pulled tight on the string, and the stick was tied fast against the circle. In a few minutes Jeff came down to the landing, and they pulled the fish box out of the water. Pa took a fish out of the box, ran the spike through its gills and out its mouth, and then let it slide down against the stick. He handed the spike to Jeff, and as he would take the fish out of the box, Jeff would string them. When they had finished, they put the fish back into the box, closed the lid, tied the end of the string to a bush on the bank, and shoved the box back into the water. Jeff took his knife and started cleaning one of the large buffalo he had left out for their supper, and Pa went back into the house.

Jeff was washing the fish in the bayou, when he saw Skeeter coming toward him in the skiff. When he pushed in at the landing, Jeff saw three large water moccasins lying in the bottom. Their heads had been neatly popped from their bodies. Skeeter threw the snakes on the bank and got out of the skiff.

"I'll give you one of these skins to trade in town tomorrow if'n you'll help me clean 'em," he said.

"I'll shore do hit," said Jeff, "cause I need somethin' of my own fer to trade. Whut you reckon them folks do with these here skins, Skeeter?"

"I heard that they makes belts and purses out of 'em."

"Well, I shore wouldn't want no snakeskin hangin' aroun' my belly or in my pocket," said Jeff.

Jeff put the cleaned fish on the grass and grasped the tail of one of the snakes. Skeeter took the other end and ran the sharp blade of his knife down the underside of the snake. When they had split the snake in half, they trimmed the meat and bones from the skin. Then Skeeter washed it in the water. When they finished cleaning all three of the snakes, they hung the skins over a limb of a tree to dry, and went into the house. Ma was giving Pa instructions as to what to bring from town the next day. Jeff took the bar of yellow soap from the shelf and went up the bayou to take a bath, and Skeeter stood at the door looking after him.

"Why air hit that Jeff's been takin' a bath afore we go to town the last few times?" asked Skeeter. "I can't see no use in him gettin' all that fancy."

"I've heard that he's sparkin' some gal in town," said Pa.

"Yeh, and he better stop that sparkin' aroun' them town girls afore he gits us all in trouble," said Ma. "You know dern well whut them folks thinks of the likes of Jeff, and they ain't no use askin' fer yore head to be chopped off."

"Whut's sparkin' mean, Ma?" asked Theresa.

"Hit's jest as well you don't know and don't never find out. They ain't no end to a woman's troubles after a man comes sniffin' around her like she were a bitch dog in heat."

"Now, I wouldn't go so fer as to say that," said Pa. "You ain't did too bad fer yoreself."

"You call livin' in this swamp and bein' treated like a nigger by all the other white folks ain't so bad? Sometimes I think we would uv been better off if'n we would have stayed in the fields. Hit's been nigh on a year now since me and Theresa has seen airy other white folks, excusin' you and the boys."

Skeeter and Theresa couldn't understand what it was their folks were arguing about. They had seen these little spats before, and they always felt sorry for Pa, but they couldn't understand why Ma didn't love living on the river as they did. Skeeter couldn't stand the thought of not being around the swamp, and he liked not having other folks around them all the time.

"Jest the same," said Ma, "you better tell the boy to watch himself while he's messin' aroun' in that town."

"Leave the boy be," said Pa, as he walked to the front porch and sat down. Ma and Theresa started cooking the supper. After a while Jeff came in, and they all sat at the table and ate in silence. When they had finished, Pa and the boys sat on the front porch, while Ma and Theresa washed the dishes and cleaned the kitchen. When the work was finished, the family went to bed, for they all knew that they had to be up long before daybreak to start preparations for the trip to town.

A few hours after dark Pa was awakened by a loud splashing coming from the bayou. Jeff and Skeeter had heard the disturbance also and were pulling on their clothes. They went to the kitchen and lighted a torch and all three went down to the landing. They could hear the splashing continuing up the bayou. The fish box had been knocked from the water and was lying several feet up on the bank. They put it back into the water and stood for a few minutes in silence and could hear the noises continue past the end of the bayou and into the swamp.

"Whut in the world do you reckon that were?" asked Pa.

"Hit beats me," said Jeff. "I never heard of a critter pullin' a stunt like that there."

Skeeter didn't say a word because he thought he knew what had caused the disturbance and knocked the box out of the water.

THREE

SKEETER WAS AWAKENED by the smell of frying fish and corn pone coming from the kitchen. He jumped out of bed, pulled on his overalls and went into the kitchen. Pa and Jeff were already up and had gone down to the landing. Ma was cooking the fish and corn pone for their lunch on the trip to town, and Theresa was cooking grits and flapjacks for their breakfast. The smell of the coffee boiling made him hungry. He walked out onto the back stoop and breathed deeply of the fresh morning air. The sky was still pitch dark, and Pa and Jeff were loading the boat by torchlight. In a few minutes they had finished and they came back to the kitchen. Jeff was dressed in his best suit of brown khaki, and his hair was slicked back with water. Pa had on a pair of clean overalls, his best blue shirt, and his big black hat. Skeeter looked at them and grunted with displeasure. He was dressed in his same dirty overalls and was without shoes.

Ma finished cooking the lunch and wrapped it in a piece of soiled brown paper. They sat down and ate the breakfast of grits and flapjacks with thick brown molasses. When they had finished, they took the lunch and went down to the boat landing, and Ma and Theresa followed them. Pa sent Skeeter back to the house to get the two croaker sacks that they used to bring their supplies home in. Pa and Jeff turned the bow of the boat down the bayou and tied the skiff on behind. Skeeter was to ride in the boat alone and guide it with an oar, with Pa and Jeff in the skiff tied behind. This was done to reduce the weight in the boat because Skeeter weighed less. After everything was loaded, Skeeter got the snakeskins and put them in his pocket. Ma was giving them a few last-minute instructions about not forgetting the supplies, and when she finished, they shoved the boat down the bayou. It was hard work for Skeeter to tow the heavy load in the bayou, but when the boat was caught in the swift water of the river, all he had to do was sit and guide with the oar. It was nearly as much fun as being in the swamp.

They had just reached the river when the eastern sky was filled with the gray streaks of dawn. The air was fresh and sharp, and Skeeter trailed one foot in the cool water. Pa and Jeff relaxed in the skiff for the pleasant ride. Life on the river wasn't really so bad, thought Pa.

It was not yet midmorning when they reached the boat docks of Mill Town, a small town of about four hundred people. It had been named Mill Town because of the sawmill on the bank of the river, and the only time the steamboats stopped was when there was lumber on the docks for them to pick up or a passenger to get on or off. There was one street of business houses, two churches, a school, and the rest were residential houses or shacks along the river. There was a Baptist and a Catholic church, because many of the people who worked at the mill were French Catholics, and some of them could not speak English.

Along the business street there were several dry-goods stores, a post office, a fish market, two saloons and a barbershop. The south end of town along the river was the

Negro quarters. The best of the townspeople lived to the north and away from the river. None of the Coreys had ever been in that part of town.

Skeeter tied the anchor line to a piling, and Pa pulled the skiff alongside and tied it to the boat. Pa and Jeff got on the dock, and Skeeter handed them the fish line. Then he climbed up and helped. It was all they could do for the three of them to lift the string of fish to the dock. Pa put the lunch inside his shirt and Jeff took the croaker sacks, and they started carrying the fish to the market. Skeeter thought his arms would break before they finally arrived.

The man who ran the market was named Mr. Blanch, a short, fat man with jet black hair. He talked with a city accent and did not look like a native of that part of the country. They had heard tales that he was from somewhere up north and had moved down here for his health. He was the only man in Mill Town that treated Pa Corey with decency.

When they arrived at the back door of the market, he opened the door for them. "Well, come on in, Abner," he said. "You are certainly a welcome sight. This is the first fish I've had in two days. All the other men said that the gar have been so bad this week that they haven't managed to catch enough for their own families to eat."

"How much air you payin' this week?" asked Pa.

"With the supply so short, I'll pay you ten cents a pound if it's good fish."

It was all Pa and the boys could do to keep from shouting with glee. They hadn't felt so good in all their lives. Mr. Blanch started examining the fish and putting them on the large scales. He felt and smelled each one as he took it from the string. "You sure got a nice one here," he said, when he came to the large cat they had caught on the trotline.

"Yessah," said Pa, "and that bugger shore give us one heck uv a time afore we got him in the boat."

Mr. Blanch turned to Pa and said: "You've got exactly four hundred and ten pounds of first-class fish here, Mr. Corey. At ten cents a pound that will amount to forty-one dollars."

He walked over to the cash drawer and took out four tens and a one dollar bill and handed them to Pa.

"I shore thank you, Mr. Blanch," said Pa.

"And I thank you, too, Abner. If you have any more next week, bring them to me. Your fish are always fresh, and I like that."

Pa and the boys walked out the front door of the market and down the street, their heads held a little high.

"That's the most money I've seed in a long time," said Jeff.

"I guess the good Lord must have heard my prayer the other day and showered this goodness down on us," said Pa.

"Kin I have a nickel fer some likker sticks?" asked Skeeter.

"Let's go to the store and git the supplies fust and see how much we has left," said Pa, "then we kin tell how much each kin have to do whut he wants to with."

They walked to the big supply store on the first corner and went inside. A clerk at the counter looked at them with contempt, but when Pa took the bills out of his pocket, the clerk immediately grabbed a pencil and started writing down his order for supplies. When Pa finished, the clerk told him that it would take better than an hour to fill the order, so Pa paid him and they went back outside. Pa had several bills and coins left in his hand. He put the bills in his pocket and handed Jeff and Skeeter fifty cents apiece. He took the lunch from his shirt, and they sat on the porch of the store and started eating.

"If'n hit's goin' to be a good whiles afore that clerk gits our supplies ready, why don't we jest meet back here in front of the store, Pa?" said Skeeter. "I wants to go see Uncle Jobe a whiles afore we has to start back."

"Now who in tarnation is Uncle Jobe?" asked Pa.

"He's a ole nigger friend uv mine down in the quarters. Me and him always visits when I gits the chance. He's the one I'm goin' to git to give me the potion fer the gars."

"Well, I guess that be a right good idea at that," said Pa. "We'll jest all meet back here in about two hours. Now don't nary one of you be no later than that. You know how Ma feels 'bout us comin' in home too late."

They finished eating the cold fish and corn pone, and each walked off in a different direction. Skeeter headed south towards the Negro quarters, Jeff headed north towards the store that Clarise Smith worked in, and Pa headed across the street towards the River Side Saloon. All three looked forward to a pleasant two hours.

Skeeter walked down the dusty lane that led to the Negro section of town. Most of the shacks were built along the river so that outhouses were not needed. They were built of cull scraps from the mill and were in much worse condition than even the Corey house. Skeeter walked to a one-room shack where the old Negro known as Uncle Jobe lived alone. Most folks said that the Negro did not know his own age, but he must have been at least ninety years old. His hair was white as silver, and his face was wrinkled with old age. The only means he had of keeping body and soul together was selling the different potions he made to the other Negroes and some white people. He had a potion for almost every ill known to mankind, and some people swore by him and would seek the advice of no other. The old man was sitting on the front porch when Skeeter arrived. When he recognized the boy, he stood up and motioned him in.

"How be ye, Massah Skeeter?" he asked. "Welcome back agin."

"I'm shore mighty proud to see you," said Skeeter, "and I done brought you a little present that I caught in the swamp."

Skeeter took one of the snakeskins out of his pocket and handed it to the old Negro. He turned it over and examined it and stroked it with his hands. "How did you ever figger that I has always wanted one of these big snakeskins?" he asked. "This is jest about the best thing anybody done ever give old Uncle Jobe."

"I shore am glad you likes hit," said Skeeter. "I was afeered you wouldn't."

"Don't you be afeered that old Uncle Jobe won't like anything that you brings him. I jest wishes they were more white boys like you aroun' to visit with me."

"Uncle Jobe," said Skeeter, "I shore wants you to do somethin' fer me if'n you kin."

"Why you knows that I'd do most airy thing fer you that air in my limits, Massah Skeeter. Now whut is hit you wants?"

"We bin havin' a heap of trouble with them dern gar messin' with our traps and lines lately. I heard that they was a potion that would keep them critters from messin' around with any hooks."

"Why, you is sho' right," said Uncle Jobe. "I have jest what you wants right here in the house. I'll git hit fer you."

Uncle Jobe got up and walked into the dim interior of the shack with Skeeter close behind him. One complete wall of the shack was shelves filled with bottles of different colored fluids. The old Negro looked through several bottles and selected a small one with a dark yellow liquid inside. Then he walked back and sat on the porch.

"This air jest whut you wants," he said. "You jest put a drap of this stuff on each bait as you fixes yore lines, and you sho' won't be bothered with no gar no more."

"I shore don't know how to thank you well enough fer this," said Skeeter. "I know Pa is goin' to be real proud when he sees hit."

"Jest you don't forget that old Uncle Jobe will help you ary time hits in his power to do so, so'es you jest bring yore problems to me and we'll see whut' we kin do abouts fixin' 'em."

They sat in silence for a long time enjoying each other's company. They seemed to understand that being together and sharing their problems was enough to satisfy each other. Finally Skeeter realized that it would soon be time to go. He hated the thought of time going by so quickly, for he would like to sit with Uncle Jobe the rest of the afternoon.

"Uncle Jobe," he said, "they's one more thing I would like to ask you about afore I has to go."

"Well, you jest go right ahead, Massah Skeeter."

"Whut kin you do about a critter in the swamp that has gone plum crazy? Hit ain't really his fault, but somethin' done happen to him that has caused him to plum lose his mind."

"Whut makes you ask me a question like that? I've heard of folks doin' that, but I ain't never heard of a critter goin' crazy. Leastwise, I sho' wouldn't like to be aroun' when that happens."

"Oh, hit ain't nothin' really, I guess. I jest wanted to ask and see."

"Well, that's one thing that I can't give you no answer on."

"I speck I better be goin' now," said Skeeter, "cause Pa tole me not to be late in gettin' back."

"If'n that's whut yore Pa said, you better be on yore way. Don't forget to come and see me agin, Massah Skeeter."

"Good-by, Uncle Jobe."

Skeeter walked back down the lane towards town, and when he reached the store, neither Pa nor Jeff was waiting for him. He went into the store and walked to the counter. When the clerk came to him, he pulled the other snakeskin from his pocket. "How much in trade will you give me fer this?" he asked.

The clerk took the snakeskin and examined it. Then he walked to a room in back of the store and stayed gone for a few minutes. He returned without the skin. "What did you want to trade it for?"

"I wants to trade hit fer some likker sticks," said Skeeter.

"We'll give you five sticks for it," said the clerk.

"That sounds like a pretty fair trade. I guess I'll jest take you up on hit."

The clerk reached under the counter and laid five of the black licorice sticks in Skeeter's hand. Skeeter put one of them in his mouth and the rest in his pocket, and went back out and sat on the porch. Pa and Jeff still were not in sight.

Skeeter sat in the warm sun and watched the wagons rolling into town. The people were coming in from the swamps and hills to do their Saturday buying and to talk with neighbors they hadn't seen for a week. The mill had shut down at noon, and little groups of men were beginning to gather on the street. There was a lot of noise coming from the saloon across the street. Now and then Skeeter thought he could hear Pa's voice sound out in loud laughter. He remembered that he still had the fifty cents in his pocket, but decided to wait and spend it some other time. He looked across the street and saw Pa come out the saloon door. Pa had a bottle in one hand and weaved back and forth as he crossed the street. As he looked at Skeeter his eyes were a little hazy.

"Where's Jeff?" he asked. "Hain't he got back yit?"

"I ain't seed him, Pa," said Skeeter.

"Well hit's time we got started back towards the house."

Pa uncorked the bottle, took a deep drink, and started to sit down. A loud noise sounded up the street, and Jeff sailed out the door of a store and landed on the wood platform in front. Three men a little larger than he were on top of him immediately, kicking and hitting with their fists. Pa recognized them as the brothers of Clarise Smith. "So that's who he were sparkin'," said Pa. "Skeeter, you go on in the store and start gittin' them supplies down to the boat as soon as you kin."

Skeeter ran into the store and started carrying supplies to the boat. Pa put the bottle in his back pocket and weaved slowly up the street. The brothers had Jeff in the dust and were kicking him with their feet. Clarise was standing in front of the store yelling for them to stop.

"Ain't no yellow-bellied swamp rat goin' to spark around my sister!" said one of the brothers.

"Let's kill the low-down son of a bitch!" said another.

Jeff was fighting back as best he could, but he was no match for the three men. People were running down the street to watch the fight. There was already a big circle formed around the men. Blood was running from Jeff's mouth, and he wasn't fighting back as hard. Pa walked through the circle of people and grabbed one of the brothers by the arm.

"Now jest a minute," he said. "You boys air goin' to kill that boy if'n all of you don't stay off him at one time."

"Air you his Pa?" asked the man.

"I shore air," said Pa, "and I aim to see that you all don't beat on him like that. Hit ain't nearbouts a fair fight."

The man drew back his fist, and before Pa could say another word, he hit Pa full strength in the eye. Pa flipped backwards and rolled through the people in the crowd. Clarise ran through the crowd and stood in the middle of her brothers.

"Now ain't you a big bunch of bullies," she cried, "beatin' up a boy and a pore ole man. If you don't stop this right now I'll never speak to none of you no more."

"Well, we'll let him go fer now," said one of the brothers, "but if'n we ever ketch the son of a bitch hangin' around here again we'll shore bust his brains out."

The three brothers walked away down the street, and the crowd began to fade away. Pa rose slowly to his feet, picked up his hat and walked over to Jeff. He took Jeff by the arm and pulled him to his feet. His mouth was badly bruised and both eyes were nearly closed.

"Air ye hurt bad, Son?" asked Pa.

"Naw, I guess I'll live."

Clarise was still standing there looking at him. They looked at each other for a few moments without speaking.

"I'm sorry," she said.

"Hit's all right," said Jeff. "Don't you worry none. I'll be back."

He turned and followed Pa toward the boat docks. When they got there, Skeeter was standing by the boat, and half the supplies were in the boat and half were in the skiff.

"Did ye git 'em all?" asked Pa.

"I shore did," said Skeeter, "and hit took me four trips. You two air a sight fer sore eyes."

They all climbed down into the boat. Pa and Jeff leaned over the side and washed their faces in the river.

"Air ye able to row, Jeff?" asked Pa.

"I guess I kin make hit all right. If'n I can't, I'll let you know."

They put the oars in the locks, Pa untied the line from the piling, and the boat floated out into the river. Jeff and Skeeter bent their arms to the oars, and the boat started upstream. Pa sat in the bow and uncorked the bottle. About halfway home the whiskey was gone, and he was sound asleep. He was still asleep when they reached the landing. Skeeter shook him to wake him, and he jumped to his feet and shouted: "Leave me at the sons of bitches!" His feet slipped in the boat and he fell backwards into the bayou. He came up sputtering and spitting water, and fighting for the bank. His hat was still on his head.

"Now ain't you a pretty sight," said Ma. "If'n you spent the money and didn't git all them supplies, you jest better git in the boat and head back to town."

"If'n you'll jest wait and see whut all I done brought you won't be fussin' at me none," said Pa.

"Whut's done happened to you and Jeff?" asked Theresa.

"Some of them mill hands tried to steal the boat and we got in a big fight," said Pa. "But we shore got the best of them."

Skeeter looked at his Pa but didn't say anything. They all gathered up bundles and went into the house. Jeff went to bed, while the rest of the family gathered in the kitchen.

"Jest look whut all I got," said Pa, and he started pulling things out of the sacks. "They's a bag of corn meal, a bag of sugar, a can of coffee, a sack of grits, a jug of molasses, a side of salt pork, a sack of okra, tomatoes, and celery stalks. That's fer the gumbo. And I also got some seed corn, some okra, tomato, collard, and radish seeds, and a sack of hog feed. Here's two bottles of snuff fer you, Ma, and a big comb fer Theresa, and a bolt of red cloth big enouf to make you and Theresa a new dress. And I also got me some gunpowder and shot. And whut do you think of this?" he said, holding up a small paper bag. "Hit's a dozen hen eggs fer us to eat."

Ma and Theresa were almost wild with excitement. Theresa ran the comb through her hair time and time again. Ma felt the cloth and then the snuff bottles. She was so happy she was about to cry.

"Now tell me, Abner," she said, "how did you git all this?"

"We had four hundred and ten pounds of the fish, and they was payin' ten cents a pound. I still got a little money left fer a rainy day."

They put up the supplies, and Ma put away the cloth and started some supper. Jeff didn't come out to eat, and Pa said to just leave him alone. They were all tired, so they didn't sit around long after supper. Skeeter and Theresa went to bed, and Theresa took the comb with her. As soon as Ma finished the dishes, she grabbed Pa by the arm and pulled him towards the bed.

"You jest come on now, Abner Corey," she said. "Me and you is goin' to imagaine we is twenty years younger than we is."

Night settled on the Corey family, and all was well except in Jeff's heart.

FOUR

THE SUN WAS ABOVE the trees when the Corey household came to life the next morning. It was Sunday, and there were no traps to check and no trotline to run. Pa didn't believe in fishing on the Sabbath, so Sunday was always a day of rest, and each member of the family could do as he pleased.

Theresa was slicing the pork side into thin, even strips while Ma was mixing flapjack batter. When the aroma of frying bacon drifted through the house, the Corey men began to arise, and Pa and Skeeter were soon in the kitchen. After the bacon was fried, Ma dropped the eggs into the hot grease, and put on fresh coffee to boil. When the eggs were done, she dropped in the flapjacks. In a few minutes she set the breakfast of fried eggs, flapjacks, bacon, molasses, and coffee on the table. Jeff was still in bed.

"You better go in there and git that boy up and make him eat some breakfast," said Ma. "He didn't eat no supper last night, and if'n he don't git somethin' in his belly, he'll shore be sick."

Pa went into the room and shook Jeff's shoulder. Jeff stirred from the bed and put on his clothes. Both eyes were almost closed, and his lips were swollen badly out of shape. His side was so sore he could hardly walk to the kitchen. He sat down at the table with the rest of the family, but the sight of food made him run to the back stoop and retch in the yard. He went back and lay down on the bed.

"I'm shore sorry that he has to be sick, with us sech a breakfast as this on the table," said Pa. "We'll have to save these other eggs till he's able to eat again."

"I'll make him a poultice after breakfast and take that swellin' out'n his face," said Ma. "And if'n Skeeter kin git me some sassafras roots, I kin make him some tea that will fix up that sore belly of his afore he knows hit."

"Well, I shore hope he won't be laid up too long," said Pa, "cause the work will be mighty hard fer me and Skeeter here to do."

"I hain't worried 'bout hit, Pa," said Skeeter. "I believe we kin manage fer a few days."

"Well, as soon as we git through eatin', you go look fer them roots," said Ma, "and, Theresa, you go git me some fresh poke salat and a few dead magnolia leaves, and I'll need a little black mud from the bayou."

They finished breakfast, and Skeeter brought in a bucket of fresh water for Ma to do the dishes with.

When Skeeter returned, Ma took the sassafras roots and put them in some water to boil. She added a pinch of salt and a small pod of red pepper. The steam from the pot filled the room with a bitter smell.

Then she started making the poultice. She tore the poke salat leaves into small pieces and put them in a pot. She crumpled the dry, brown magnolia leaves on top of them. She put in a handful of the black bayou mud and three handfuls of ashes from the hearth, added a cup of water, stirred the mixture, and put it over the hearth to heat.

When the sassafras had boiled until the water turned red, she poured out a cup and took it to Jeff.

"Now you jest hold yore nose and drink this," she said, "cause hit'll cure jest about ary thing known to man."

Jeff raised up in the bed and drank the hot tea. He had to hold his hand over his mouth to keep from throwing it up on the floor. Ma went back to the kitchen and brought in the pot of hot poultice. Jeff lay back on the bed, and she put a thick layer of the substance over his face.

"That will draw the swellin' out afore you knows hit," she said. "You'll be jest as good as new in a day or so."

She went back to the kitchen and started cleaning the crawfish for the gumbo dinner. She peeled the husk and heads from them, saving only the tails. Pa was sitting on the back stoop whittling on a stick.

"Abner," said Ma, "they's a powerful lot of crawfish here fer jest the few of us, and they won't keep no longer. Why don't we take all the fixin's and row up to the Hookers' and go neighborin', and I could fix hit up there. They's plenty fer everbody, and me and Theresa would shore enjoy hit. Hit's been nigh on a year since we been neighborin' with them."

"Do ye think hit would be all right to leave Jeff here by hisself?" asked Pa.

"I think hit would do him good to be able to rest without no noise abouts. And I kin fix him some broth to eat if'n he gits hongry."

"Well, I guess hit's all right with me," said Pa, "but you better hurry up and let's git goin'. Hit's a fer piece up there."

Ma and Theresa finished the housework and started dressing. Ma put on her old black dress and her hat with the big red feather on top. Theresa wore her snug-fitting, white cotton dress, and combed her flaming red hair until it looked like silk hanging down her back. Pa dressed in his best overalls and shirt and wore his black hat.

When they were dressed, Ma went into the room with Jeff and made him drink another cup of hot tea.

"We're goin' neighborin' up to the Hookers'," she said, "so'es you jest stay in bed and rest. They's a pot of broth on the hearth fer you to eat if'n you gits hongry. You leave that poultice on till this afternoon and then take hit off and put on a new one. And if'n yore belly don't git better soon, git you some more of that tea in there and drink hit."

Jeff didn't say anything, but nodded his head to show that he understood. They put the fixin's for the dinner in the bow to keep dry; Pa and Skeeter sat in the middle to row, and Ma and Theresa sat in the rear. The boat sank a little deep on the side where Ma was sitting. They shoved off down the bayou.

The Hooker family lived five miles up the river from the Coreys. They were swamp rats, but they did not make their living in the same way as the Coreys. They made whiskey and took it to Mill Town and Fort Henry to sell. There was good money in the whiskey trade, so they were always fixed better than the Coreys.

Cline and Bertha Hooker had ten sons, with ages ranging from sixteen to thirty. They were unusually large people, and even the youngest of the Hooker boys was as large as Pa or Jeff. Old Man Hooker was more than six feet tall and weighed over two hundred pounds, and even though he was ten years older than Pa Corey, his hair was still jet black, as was that of all his sons. There were legends told about them all the way from Jackson to New Orleans, and it had been told that they had once cornered a giant black bear and killed it with their bare hands. Everyone had heard of the Hooker brothers, and all men feared them.

The first of the Hooker boys had been born twins, and they were named Sun Up and Sun Down. Then in succession came High Noon, Low Twelve, Quarter Moon, Half Moon,

Fourth Moon, Full Moon, and No Moon. The night their last son was born the sparks from the fire nearly burned the house down, so they named him Sparky. He was the best looking of the lot. All but Sparky wore black beards to match their hair, but he had not yet begun to shave.

The Coreys reached the mouth of the cove that led to the Hooker house and turned the boat toward the landing. The Hookers' house was not set as far back as the Coreys', and they could see the river from their front porch. When the boat touched the landing, several hounds raced to the bank and barked madly. Old Man Hooker walked down from the house.

"Well, I'll be a dad-burned 'gator's uncle," he said, "if'n hit ain't the Coreys. Git out and come in the house. Hit's been a coon's age since we've seed you folks."

"We're shore glad to see you too," said Pa. "We come up to neighbor a spell today."

They got out of the boat and walked to the house. Ma brought the fixin's with her. Skeeter was scared of the dogs, so he stayed close to Pa. They climbed the steep steps and went in.

"Jest look who's come, Bertha," said the old man.

"Well, dog, if'n hit ain't the Coreys," she said. "I was jest about to believe that you folks had died or moved off."

The only one of the Hooker boys who was in the house was the youngest, Sparky. When Theresa came in, he stared at her with his mouth open, and she flushed and stared back. She had never had a boy look at her like that. The old man brought in chairs, and they all sat down.

"Don't jest stand there like a tomcat, Sparky," he said. "Go out to the kitchen and git us a jug of that best whiskey so'es we kin offer our guests a little nip."

Skeeter stared wide-eyed at the Hookers' collection of guns in the room. One solid wall was covered with guns. Skeeter didn't think that there were that many guns in the whole world. The old man saw him staring so he said to Skeeter: "You kin go look at them closer if'n you want to, but jest be careful, cause all them things air loaded."

Skeeter got up and went over to have a closer look. Sparky came back with a gallon jug of the white whiskey and handed it to the old man as he pulled out the corncob stopper.

"Take ye a good snort, Abner," he said. "That's the best white lightnin' that's made on Pearl River."

Pa took a deep drink and handed the jug back to the old man. Then the old man handed the jug to Ma.

"I'll jest take a little nip," she said. "I'm always afeered to take much afore dinner."

She took a short drink and passed the jug on to Ma Hooker. The old woman turned it up and took a deeper drink than Pa Corey. Then the jug was passed on to the old man, and he repeated the performance.

"They ain't nothin' like a good snort of white lightnin' to warm a person's belly and make him feel neighborly," he said.

"I done brought all the fixin's to make up a big pot of my special crawfish gumbo," said Ma, "so'es we better go on in the kitchen and git it started. Hit takes a long whiles fer it to git jest right."

The two women got up and went to the kitchen, and Theresa followed. Sparky was still staring at her. When she looked at him, it gave her a funny feeling.

"Where's yore other boy, Abner?" asked the old man.

"He's laid up in the bed at home. He got in a big fight down at Mill Town yestiddy and got beat up somethin' awful. Them three Smith boys down there jumped him cause he were sparkin' aroun' their sister. I run to help him, and that's how I got this busted eye I'm totin' aroun' with me."

"That weren't much of a fair fight, were hit? I'll tell my boys about that next time they goes to Mill Town."

"I shore wish they could git back on them Smith boys," said Pa. "They called us sons of bitches jest cause we lives on the river."

"Well, if'n they ever calls one of my boys that we'll pull down their pants and whop their butts till they looks like the sun comin' over the river."

They passed the jug again, and both took long draughts of the whiskey.

"Derned if'n that little gal of yorn ain't turned out to be a pretty thing," said the old man. "They ain't nothin' on the river whut looks as good as she do, and from the way Sparky's mouth air hangin' open, I believe he done taken a liken fer her."

In the kitchen the two women were preparing the dinner. Ma chopped up the okra, tomatoes, and celery stalks into a big iron pot. She dropped in a few small pods of red pepper, and added garlic and wild sage. Then she put in the crawfish tails and filled the pot with water and set it on the stove to simmer.

"I shore would like to have a nice stove like this," said Ma.

"Hit takes one that big to cook the rations fer a big bunch of overgrown hogs like I got stayin' aroun' here," said the old woman.

"I don't see how come hit don't near 'bouts kill you keepin' house fer so many men," said Ma. "Hit's all I kin do with jest three and Theresa to help me."

"Hit do nearbouts git a pore ole soul like me down sometimes," she said, "but I guess I'm jest used to hit."

Pa Corey and the old man went through the kitchen and out the back door to go look at the whiskey still. Skeeter followed them, but Sparky stayed inside so he could watch Theresa.

"I want you to see these new boats we air buildin'," said the old man. "They's made out of planed cypress and is put together with screws, and we's almost done with them."

They walked up to where the two boats were sitting on props. They were more than twice as long as the Coreys' boat and much deeper. There were two seats in the middle and locks for four oars instead of two. Pa had never seen boats like these before.

"Them shore air fine," he said. "Them's abouts the best I've ever seed."

"Hit won't take us no time to run in a load of whiskey in them boats," said the old man. "I'd near 'bout bet that when four of them boys sets behind them oars they can near 'bout outrun a steamboat."

He took Pa on through the woods to show him the still. The whole still was set high off the ground on pilings to protect it during the floods. The floor was made of thick cypress planking, and the roof was better than the Coreys had over their house. They had built it on the bank of a creek, so it would be near fresh water.

The Hooker boys were sitting around the still, and when Pa Corey came up they all gave him a greeting. Pa and the old man looked around for a few minutes and then went on to see the garden. Skeeter stayed behind to watch the workings of the still.

After he had looked at everything, he walked up to Sun Up and said, "I've got a potion to home that will keep gars from messin' with baits and gittin' in traps."

"Did you hear that, boys," he laughed. "He says he got some kind of potion to home."

"Let's give him a big snort," said No Moon.

Three of them grabbed Skeeter and held him on the floor. No Moon came over and forced some whiskey down Skeeter's throat. It burned like someone had put fire in his belly.

"Jest look at him," said Sun Up. "The little bugger looks like he's drunk already. We better sober him up."

They jerked Skeeter's overalls off and carried him to the side of the platform and threw him into the creek. He came up spitting water and fighting for the bank. He climbed up the bank and came back on the platform to put on his clothes. Pa and the old man came back just as Skeeter was thrown into the creek. The old man ran up to the boys.

"Now, air that any way fer you boys to be treatin' a guest of ourn," he said. "You ought to be plum ashamed of yore-selves."

"We's just havin' a little fun with him," said Sun Up. "We didn't aim to hurt him none."

"They ain't hurt me none," said Skeeter. He was kind of proud that he had been thrown in the creek by the Hooker boys. That would be something good to tell Uncle Jobe.

"Well, jest the same," said the old man, "if'n I ketch you doin' hit agin, I'll take me a stick and stir up a lot of brains."

Pa and the old man walked back toward the house, while Skeeter put his clothes on. He wanted to stay around and be with the boys.

"Whut you totin' that big knife fer?" asked Sun Down.

"I uses hit in the swamp sometimes," said Skeeter.

"Bet you couldn't hit the side of a barn with hit," said Sun Down.

"Bet a dollar he kin," said No Moon.

"That's a bet," said Sun Down.

They reached into their pockets, and each pulled out a dollar bill, throwing it on the platform floor. Sun Down took a cigarette paper from his pocket, spit on it, and stuck it to one of the posts holding up the roof. "Let's see him hit that," he said.

"That ain't no fair trial," said No Moon. "He couldn't hit that with a rifle."

"You kin back out on yore bet if'n you want to," said Sun Down. He knew that No Moon wouldn't back down because no Hooker had ever been known to back out on a bet already made. He also thought that he had tricked No Moon out of a dollar.

They drew a line with a piece of burned stick about ten feet from the paper, and they told Skeeter to stand there and not cross the line.

"I think I'll jest back up a little bit if'n you don't mind," said Skeeter. He walked all the way to the far end of the platform and turned around. It was sixty feet from the paper.

"Now jest look at that," said No Moon. "You and Sun Down must have had this made up. You jest tryin' to beat me out'n a dollar."

Skeeter drew back the knife, hesitated a moment, and sent it flying through the air. The point of the blade pinned the paper to the post. They all looked at Skeeter with amazement. No Moon danced around wildly and picked up the money.

Sun Down reached in his pocket, took out another cigarette paper, and stuck it to the post. He pulled the knife out and handed it to Skeeter.

"Let's see you do that again," he said.

Skeeter drew back the knife and again sent the blade into the center of the paper.

"Well, I'm damned!" said Sun Down. "This little bugger air shore good with that thing. Didn't think he could do hit."

Skeeter knew that he was in with the Hooker boys now, and that they wouldn't bother him any more. A bell rang from the back of the house, and they went up for dinner.

They went into the front room and passed around a jug while the women were putting the food on the table. Besides the gumbo there were baked sweet potatoes, dried peas, turnip roots, stewed spare ribs, and corn pone.

When they sat down at the table, the Hooker boys started grabbing plates wildly. The old man stood up and banged on the table with his fist.

"Mind yore manners with company here!" he shouted, "and put them vittles back till I turn up some thanks. You'll have the Coreys thinkin' I done raised a bunch of hogs."

They put the food on their plates back into the dishes, and lowered their heads. The old man stood up and raised his hands above him.

"Thank Ye fer these vittles," he said, "and have mercy on our pore souls. Amen." Then mayhem broke loose. There was a loud clatter of food hitting plates and forks hitting food. Conversation was out of the question during the meal, and as soon as all the food was gone, the boys got up and went back to the still to lie down and sleep. Skeeter went with them, but Sparky went to the front porch and sat down.

"That was the best crawfish I ever et in my life," said the old man. "I could have et a barrel of hit."

"I'm mighty proud you like hit," said Ma.

The women cleaned the table and went to the kitchen to wash the dishes. Pa and the old man sat down to talk. After the work in the kitchen was finished, Ma and the old woman came in and sat down to join the talk, and Theresa went out on the front porch. When she saw Sparky there, she turned and started to go back.

"Don't go back in," he said. "I been wantin' to sit and talk to you."

Theresa came over to him and sat down but didn't say anything. She didn't know what to say, because she had never talked to a boy before, except those in her family, and this was different.

"Want to see the biggest cypress tree on the river?" he asked.

"I guess I do if'n Pa and Ma don't keer."

"They don't keer if'n you do. Let's go."

They got up and went into the yard. He took her along a path that led down the river. The path was so narrow and the brush on each side so thick that only one person could walk along it at one time, so she had to follow behind him. As they walked on, the path got a little wider, and then they came out in a little clearing on the bank of the river. On the edge of the clearing there stood the tallest tree Theresa had ever seen. Looking up from the base, it seemed that the clouds were drifting through its top. Its branches were covered with moss swaying with the wind. It was beautiful standing there in its majestic silence. Theresa was thrilled.

"Pa says hit's twenty feet right through the middle," said Sparky.

"Hit's the biggest thing I've ever seed," said Theresa.

They walked over and sat down under a magnolia tree and watched the river flow by. The muddy water boiled and bubbled and left brown foam along the bank.

"You got a boy friend?" asked Sparky.

"No," said Theresa. "You got a girl friend?"

"Naw," he said. "Ain't never seed one before that I liked."

They sat in silence for a few minutes; Sparky turned and looked at her.

"You like me?"

"Yes."

He put his arms around her and drew her close to him. He ran his fingers through her long silky hair. Then he turned her face up and put his lips to hers. The bubbles on the river seemed to pop and send music through the air. Theresa had never known such a feeling. Her heart pounded madly, and the blood rushed to her head. So this was what sparking was like. She put her arms around him, and they held each other close.

"I love you," he said.

"I love you, too," said Theresa, "and I'm scared."

"You don't need to never be scared of me. I'll never do nothin' to make you scared or to harm you. And I'll never stand fer nobody else to make you that way."

They sat arm in arm and watched the water flow by. Theresa had never felt so happy in her life. She didn't believe what Ma had said when Ma had the argument with Pa.

She could not be happier, and could never be happy with anyone but Sparky.

"We better go back to the house," she said.

They got up and Sparky put his arms around her, and they kissed again. The wind played melodies through the branches of the tall cypress tree.

"Let's you and me be promised," said Sparky.

"Hit's all right with me if'n Ma and Pa say we kin."

They turned up the trail towards the house. On the way back the brush seemed much greener and the sky much brighter.

They crossed the yard, hand in hand, and went into the house. The old people were still sitting and talking. No one else was in the house, because the rest were still asleep at the still. Sparky broke in on their conversation. He turned to Ma and Pa Corey. Theresa stood beside him.

"We've got something to say to you," he said. "We want to be promised if'n you'll say hit's all right with you."

Old Man Hooker jumped to the floor and danced around and around the room. "You see, whut did I tell you!" he said. "I knowed he had takin' a likin' to her. I could tell by the way he's been lookin' moon-eyed ever since she's been here."

Ma and Pa Corey looked at each other, and Pa said, "Hit suits me jest fine. What about you, Ma?"

"I guess it suits me, too," she said. "I reckon she would be jest as good off with Sparky there as with airy other man. But I do want you both to wait a spell and git a little more age on you afore you do anything about hit."

"Did you hear that, Bertha?" shouted the old man. "Hit's all right with them. Our Sparky is promised to the best lookin' gal in Mississippi. I was jest about to think I would never be a grandpappy, with them boys turnin' their heads ever time they sees a gal. I shore air proud of them both."

The old woman was just as proud as her husband at the thought of having a beautiful girl like Theresa in the family. Pa was proud, too, much prouder than he had shown. The old man grabbed a gun from the wall and ran to the back door. He pointed it through the trees and shot it toward the still. Black-bearded men poured from the woods like bees from a hive, and swarmed toward the house.

"What air hit?" shouted Sun Up.

"Each one of you bring a jug and come on up to the house," cried the old man. "I've got news fer you."

They went back to the still and each of them grabbed a jug and came to the house. Skeeter followed behind them. They came in the front room and stood around expectantly. The old man signaled for them to be silent.

"Sparky and Theresa here are promised," he said.

He could just as well have said that the revenuers were coming. The brothers went wild. They ran around the room slapping each other on the back and slapping Sparky and passing jugs. The old man grabbed a jug and handed it to Pa and Ma Corey. They both took heavy drinks. Then fiddles and guitars were brought out, and the room was filled with music. The old man grabbed Ma Corey, and Pa grabbed the old woman and started a dance. Skeeter didn't understand what was going on so he sat in a corner to watch. Sparky and Theresa slipped out to the front porch to be alone. The jugs were passed again and again, and the old people danced until they fell exhausted to their chairs.

"We better git started towards home," said Ma. "Hit's gittin' kinda late in the afternoon."

"I guess we better at that," said Pa.

"Run put a side of pork and some sweet pertators in their boat, Sun Up," said the old man, "and put in a couple of jugs of whiskey fer Abner. I been noticin' the way old Skeeter been starin' at them guns." He walked over to the wall where the guns were and took down a small rifle. "This here's fer you, Skeeter. We'd never miss hit with all the guns we got and here's two boxes of shot fer hit, too."

The old man handed the rifle and shot to Skeeter. Skeeter stroked the barrel and turned it over and over in his hands.

"I don't know how to thank ye enough, Mr. Hooker," he said.

"You jest learn how to shoot like them boys says you kin throw that knife, and hit'll be enough fer me."

"You shouldn't be givin' us so much stuff," said Pa.

"Whut's the difference," said the old man. "We's goin' to be intermixed, ain't we?"

The Coreys walked down to the landing with the entire Hooker family following. Ma and Pa were both a little drunk. Theresa said good-by to Sparky and got in the bow of the boat. Pa and Ma sat in the middle, with Skeeter in the rear to steer with his oar on the trip back down.

"You folks has got to call more often now," said the old man.

"We will," said Pa, "and you call, too."

Skeeter shoved the boat off with his oar and paddled towards the swift water of the river. The Hookers waved good-by and went back into the house. When they reached the river, they could hear the music start up in the house again and the stomping of many feet. Sparky was still standing on the porch waving to Theresa as Skeeter turned the boat down the river towards home.

Pa looked at the pork and the potatoes and the whiskey in the boat and said: "Our little Theresa has done right well by herself, ain't she?"

"She shore has," said Ma.

The rest of the trip was made in silence, with Theresa dreaming of Sparky, Ma and Pa thinking whiskey thoughts, and Skeeter stroking the rifle with one hand.

"We should have gone neighborin' more often," said Pa.

"I guess we should at that," was the reply.

FIVE

PA WAS UP EARLY the next morning shooting squirrels around the clearing to use for fresh bait for the trotline. He killed a few extra ones for Ma to fix for dinner. Jeff was not as sick as he had been the day before, but he was still not well enough to get around much. Most of the swelling was gone from his face, and he was not sick on the stomach, but he was sore and wanted to rest another day. When Pa came in, he skinned the squirrels, cut them into pieces and put them in a bag.

When breakfast was done, Pa and Skeeter shoved off down the bayou in the boat, Skeeter taking his gar potion with him. They turned up the river and rowed to the cove where the traps were set. When they pulled up the first trap, Pa cursed loudly and slammed his fist against the side of the boat. The top netting of the trap was cut to ribbons, and there was not a fish left in it. They pulled it into the boat and went to the other one. It was not cut, and there were several small cat and buffalo in it. Pa took the fish out and pulled the trap along the side of the boat and back to the place where the first one had been set. They always caught more fish there, and he wanted to leave the good trap in that spot.

"Let me put some of this gar potion on hit afore you lower hit back," said Skeeter.

"Well, I guess hit can't hurt none," said Pa.

Skeeter rubbed some of the fluid on the mouth of the trap, and they lowered it back into the water. After they had tied the lines to the stakes, they went back down the river to the trotline. Most of the baits were gone, and two lines were cut. Two of the hooks had only the heads of fish on them, and they got one cat off the entire line. Skeeter rubbed some of the fluid on each fresh bait before Pa put it on the hook. When they finished, they rowed back home. Pa put their small catch in the fish box and carried the trap to the house, then spent the rest of the morning mending it.

Skeeter showed Jeff his new rifle and told him all about their trip to the Hookers' the day before. He didn't understand all about Theresa and Sparky, but he explained well enough for Jeff to understand what had happened.

"I'd shore ruther have them boys fer me then agin me," said Jeff. "Maybe they'll come in handy fer me sometime. Let's see how yore rifle shoots, Skeeter."

Skeeter got the rifle, and they went out to the front porch. He brought a couple of shots with him, and there was already one in the breech. There were several white cranes along the edge of the water down the bayou, so Skeeter picked one of them as his target. He pointed the sight at the feet of the crane and then raised it until it looked as if the crane was sitting on top of the sight. He pulled the trigger and the crane dropped to the water. Pa was watching while mending the trap.

"Hit shore do shoot true," said Skeeter. "I could jest about hit anything with this gun."

"Let me try hit now," said Jeff.

"Now, you boys quit shootin' them cranes," said Pa. "If'n you got to try that thing on somethin', try hit on somethin' we kin eat. Tain't no use in killin' them critters."

Jeff looked around for another target. He saw several mallard ducks swimming around in the edge of the marsh grass. He took a steady aim and pulled the trigger, and one of the ducks slumped over in the water. The other ducks did not fly away.

"I got one more shot here," said Skeeter, "so let me try hit again."

He took the rifle, loaded it, and sighted it at a duck. His aim was true, and another one slumped in the water.

"Now you boys jest go git them ducks and clean 'em fer Ma to fix fer dinner," said Pa. "We kin keep them squirrels I cleaned fer bait tomorrow. I'd heap ruther eat them ducks."

Skeeter got in the skiff, poled down the bayou, and brought back the ducks. They were plump and fat from their winter feeding. The Coreys seldom ever shot the ducks because they could not spare the shot. Skeeter and Jeff picked and cleaned them and took them in to Ma to bake for dinner, then they went back to the porch and sat in the sun.

"We goin' deer huntin' over in the woods tomorrow, Pa?" asked Skeeter.

"I guess we better wait till Wednesday fer Jeff to git a little better fust," he said. "Me and you wouldn't be able to tote one of them big critters out of the woods by ourselves."

"Why is hit that they's woods on that side of the river and swamp on this un, Pa?" asked Skeeter.

"I guess that's the way the good Lord wanted hit to be," said Pa. "He made all kind of critters on this river and they all has to have a home. The deer and bear and turkey and critter sech as that can't live in no swamp, so He made the woods fer them to roam in. And He made the woods high so the river couldn't come in during the floods and drown 'em. And then the frogs and the snakes and 'gators couldn't live in the woods so He made the swamp fer them. He's made a place for all folks and critters, and will look out fer them if'n they'll jest stay in their place and be sotisfied."

"If'n the floods don't go into the woods like hit do here, how come you to build the house here 'stead uv in the woods?" Skeeter asked.

"I'd heap ruther have the floods come at me than have them bear messin' aroun' the house and them deer eatin' the plantins as soon as they come out of the ground," said Pa. "The Lord made them woods fer the critters, and so fer as I'm concerned, they kin have whut was made fer them all to theirselves. I'd jest as soon stay here in the swamp."

"I'd heap ruther be here, too," said Skeeter.

"You better go out behin' the house and git that old ax and sharpen hit real good," said Pa. "Me and you have got to clear a little piece of ground this afternoon fer yore Ma and Theresa to set out them new seeds I got. Hit'll be full moon in a couple of days, and if'n they ain't set out then, they won't be no use to set 'em out at all."

Skeeter brought the ax to the porch and started sharpening it on the old whet rock. He rubbed it along the blade until the ax was as sharp as a razor. Ma came to the porch and called them to dinner.

After dinner, Pa and Skeeter started clearing a place for the new garden. Pa would chop away the brush and small trees and Skeeter would put them in a pile. When all the brush was cut away, Pa dug up the roots with a hoe, while Skeeter pulled the weeds from the ground with his hands. The hot sun bore down on them, and sweat rolled from their bodies. Their overalls were soaked, and their bodies were covered with the black grime of the soil. When the ground was cleared, Pa took the hoe and broke the soil into long even rows. Skeeter chopped up the brush and trees and carried them to the house to use as firewood. It was late in the afternoon when they finished. They went into the house and got clean overalls and went down to the bayou, washed their clothes and themselves, then returned to the house. They were very tired and after supper went to bed.

Pa and Skeeter set out up the river early the next morning with the trap Pa had repaired, and when they reached the cove, they pulled far in to set the trap before they looked at the one already out. After they finished, they went back and pulled up the first one. There was not a fish in it, and it had not been cut by a gar.

"Well, I'll be derned," said Pa. "That's the fust time I ever seed that happen. I ain't never knowed a trap not to have a single fish in hit 'ceptin' when hit was cut."

They lowered the trap back into the water and moved on to look at the trotline. They went the entire length of the line and not a bait had been touched.

"Well, I'm derned agin," said Pa. "I ain't never seed sech a sight. Hit's that potion of yores that done this, Skeeter. Whut did that nigger say was in that stuff?"

"He didn't say, Pa," said Skeeter, "but hit shore kept them gars away, didn't hit?"

"Yeah, and everthing else, too." Pa smiled. "I guess hit's worth hit jest to fool them gars out'n a meal this one time," said Pa. "Hit's a good thing I brought this new bait with us. Now let's go back along the line and put fresh bait on all the hooks." Pa threw the old ones into the river.

"I guess the water will wash that stuff off the trap afore tonight," said Pa. "If'n hit don't, them gars shore air in fer another surprise."

When they reached home there was nothing to do, so they sat around the front porch waiting for dinner. Ma was cooking some of the pork and sweet potatoes the Hookers had given them, and the smell made Skeeter's nose twitch with delight. Pa slipped into his room and took a deep drink from one of the jugs of whiskey.

After the meal, Skeeter poled off toward the swamp in the skiff. It was late in the afternoon when he returned.

"Whut you been doin' in that swamp so long?" asked Ma.

"I been lookin' fer a critter, but I didn't find him," he said.

"Whut kind of a critter?" asked Ma.

"Jest a critter," said Skeeter, and walked out of the room.

Skeeter was so excited that it was far into the night before he could stop thinking about the approaching hunt and go to sleep. Once during the night he thought he heard something flouncing under the house but decided that he was mistaken. Thet critter wouldn't come clear to the house looking fer me, he thought, and went back to sleep.

SIX

PA CAME INTO THE ROOM and awakened Skeeter and Jeff. It was pitch dark outside, but breakfast was already on the table when they walked into the kitchen. They sat down and ate while Ma and Theresa fixed them a lunch to take along. When they finished, Skeeter went back into his room and put on his old brogans. He strapped his knife around his waist, put a box of shells in his pocket, and picked up the rifle. Pa had the shotgun and a tin of powder and shot. Jeff picked up the bag of food, and they went outside.

"You better go back inside and git us a torch, Jeff," said Pa. "Hit's so dark out here I couldn't see a nigger two feet in front uv me."

Jeff went back into the house and came out with a lighted pine knot in his hand. The light cast varied shadows along the ground in front of him. Jeff climbed into the bow of the boat to hold the torch, and Pa and Skeeter rowed them down the bayou. The air was cold, and Skeeter shivered and pulled the collar of his shirt tight around his neck.

74

They reached the place where the muddy water merged with the clear, and pointed the boat downstream.

The river looked strange and forbidden with the torch as their only light. They pulled close along the bank, and the shadows of light made the tall cypress trees look like gray ghosts in the night. It started Skeeter thinking of the night he and Jeff had been in the swamp with no light, and then he remembered the giant 'gator with the frog gig in its head, and he didn't want to think about it any more.

They drifted slowly along the bank for about a mile, and then Pa and Skeeter turned the boat into a clump of bushes hanging over the water. Jeff pulled the bow of the boat up on the bank and tied the rope to a tree. They broke limbs from trees and piled in the boat to make it impossible for anyone passing on the river to see it. Then Pa took the torch and led them away from the water.

The brush was so thick that they had to walk single file, and the last person in the line could not get the benefit of the light. Skeeter had to feel his way along in the dark and keep in the direction of the light ahead. After they had traveled a short distance away from the river, they sat down to wait for the dawn, for Pa could not find the place he wanted to go with only a torch for light. They sat on a dead log, and Pa and Skeeter loaded their guns.

In a little while the sun sent long rays of light through the tops of the tall trees. The woods seemed to take on a different appearance as the light crept in and the darkness went away. The squirrels came out of their nests and began looking for breakfast and playing in the trees. There were big black ones, red fox squirrels, gray cat squirrels, all playing together—paying no mind to the humans sitting on the ground. The woodpeckers started the rhythmical beating of their bills against the trunks of dead trees. Birds of all colors and sounds flew through the air. A covey of quail flushed from their bed for the night and went out in search of grass seeds for their food. A mother coon walked along a path leading to a water hole with her litter of little ones following. Skeeter was fascinated by the sights that he saw. He almost had a feeling of regret when Pa told him it was time to move on, but then he remembered the hunt and got up eagerly to move to the deer grounds.

The woods were very thick for a long distance away from the river, and progress through them was slow. Skeeter thought that he had never seen so many different kinds of trees. The buck vines were laced from tree to tree, and it was impossible to see more than a few feet ahead. There were cypress trees, scrub oak and big water oaks, hickory trees, holly, beech, dogwood, magnolias, pines, and dozens of other different trees, all with vines running between them. Sometimes they had to crawl on the ground to move at all.

As they got further away from the river, the woods began to thin out, and the going was not so difficult. Finally, they came into a great open stretch of pine and hickory trees. Pa showed them scars on the trees where the big bucks had rubbed their antlers. Some of the scars were fresh, and they knew that the deer had been there the night before. They found a trail that the deer were using to go to water, and Pa told Skeeter to sit on a log and watch the trail.

"If'n you see a deer comin' slow, jest wait till he's on you and aim at his fore shoulder," said Pa, "but if'n he's runnin' fast, wait till he's right at you and let out a loud whistle. He'll stop and look at you ever time, and then let him have it. If'n we hears you shoot we'll come to you, and if'n you hears us shoot you come to us. We's goin' down the trail jest a piece and wait. Now be kerful and make yore shot count."

Pa and Jeff walked down the trail and left Skeeter by the log. He leaned the gun against a tree and raked the leaves and pine straw away from the log with his hands, so that he could stand up and turn around without making any noise. He sat down and began his wait. The squirrels were in the trees above him, and he watched them at their play. They would jump from limb to limb, and hang by their feet, and chase each other up and down the trunk. When a bird would light in the trees, they would chase it away and chatter loudly while doing so. He almost went to sleep watching them.

Skeeter could sit on the log and see for a hundred yards both ways down the trail. The brush and trees were thick along the sides of it so that it would not be visible in any direction except straight down. He had almost given up hope of seeing a deer, when he heard a clanking coming down the trail. He looked and saw a big buck coming straight toward him. The buck's antlers were hitting the trees close along the trail and making the noise. It had not seen Skeeter, and it kept coming straight toward him. He cocked the hammer of his rifle and waited. Cold sweat was pouring from his face, and his heart was pounding inside him. His hands shook so that he was afraid he could not aim the gun. He thought that the deer would never reach him, but when it was directly in front of him, he aimed at the fore shoulder and pulled the trigger.

The deer leaped forward and fell to its knees. Blood was pouring from its shoulder, as it looked around and saw Skeeter for the first time. The wind had been with it, and it had not smelled him. Skeeter could see surprise in its eyes, and he hurriedly breached the gun and put in another shell. As the deer rose to its feet and started to run, Skeeter's second shot grazed its eye, and it fell again. Slowly rising to its feet, it ran off through the woods before Skeeter could load the gun again. There were two pools of blood on the ground where the deer had fallen, and a steady stream of blood followed the wounded animal through the brush. Skeeter didn't know what to do, so he sat down on the log to wait for Pa and Jeff, and in a few minutes they came running up to him.

"Did you git him?" asked Pa.

"I knocked him down twice, but he still run off through the bresh," said Skeeter. "I don't see how that critter walked with lead in him like that."

"They're powerful hard to kill sometimes," said Pa.

Pa walked over and looked at the two pools of blood and the trail of blood leading through the brush.

"That critter's hurt bad," he said. "Let's trail him. He won't git far afore he falls."

They followed the trail of blood through the brush and vines and through open places in the woods. Every few feet they came to a pool of blood on the ground where the deer had stopped to rest, and blood was smeared on the sides of trees and on vines.

"That critter's blind as a bat," said Pa. "He's runnin' into trees and vines and anything that gits in his way."

"Where you reckon he's goin', Pa?" asked Skeeter.

"He's headin' fer the nearest water hole," said Pa. "When them critters gits a hole in them they jest has a natural cravin' to lay in a pool of water. And sometimes when they ain't hurt too bad, they gits well that way. I killed a big ole buck one time with gunshot all in him, but this un will never git there. He's 'bout done now."

The stream of blood became thinner and the pools nearer together. They came through some thick buck vines and found the deer lying on the ground and bleating. When he saw them, he raised his head and tried to get up. His legs were too weak, and he fell back to the ground. Pa ran up to him and grabbed his antlers, and the deer tried to struggle away from him, but it was too weak to do so. Pa pulled out his knife and cut the buck's throat. It quivered a few minutes and then lay still.

"You shore got you a nice one fer the first time you been deer huntin'," said Pa. "He's got ten points on his antlers, and I'd say he'll weigh mighty nigh four hundred pounds. We better go ahead and git this sucker bled."

They tied one end of a rope they had brought with them to the deer's hind feet and threw the other end of the rope over a limb of a tree. Then they pulled it into the air and tied the rope to the trunk of the tree so it would stay there. Pa took his knife and split the deer down the stomach and removed all its insides. Then he let it hang for the blood to drain out. While they were waiting they took out the lunch and ate.

"We goin' to skin him here?" asked Skeeter.

"We better take him home first," said Pa, "or else the meat will git mighty dirty when we have to take him back through all them buck vines."

When they finished eating, they cut a small sweet gum tree and trimmed the limbs from it. Then they lowered the deer to the ground and tied its feet over the pole. They picked up the pole and started walking with it, but the deer's antlers dragged the ground, so they stopped and tied its antlers to the pole.

Their progress was not too hard while they were in the big woods, but as they got closer to the river and the woods grew thicker, it became more difficult. They moved very slowly and had to stop often and rest. Sometimes they had to drag the deer along the ground. Sweat poured from them, and their muscles began to ache with tiredness.

They stopped once and laid the deer down so they could rest. Just as they sat down on the ground a young buck jumped out of the buck vines in front of them. Pa could not resist the shot, so he jumped to his feet, sighted the old gun, and pulled the trigger. The blast knocked him back several feet as the shots left the barrel. The deer fell dead in its tracks, and they walked over to where it was lying. It had two antlers, about five inches long, sticking straight out of its head.

"Hit's a nice young spike buck," said Pa. "That's the best eatin' there is. Hit's a lot better than a big ole buck. We ain't fur from the river, so let's tote the big un on down to the boat and come back and git this un. We kin take this un home fer us to eat and then come back and skin the big un on the river. We kin stop the steamboat and sell hit to them, cause I've heard that they'll pay a purty good price fer venison."

Before they left, they took a piece of the rope and tied the small buck to a limb. Pa split him and left him to bleed. Then they took the big one to the river and left him, and came back and got the small one. They tied the big buck to a limb, put the small one in the boat and rowed home. When they reached home, they hung the deer from a post and left it for Ma and Theresa to skin, and went back to the place where they had left the big one. It was not long before dusk when they finished skinning the buck and heard the steamboat coming up the river. They loaded the deer and the hide into the boat and rowed out into the river. When Pa saw the steamboat coming, he stood up and waved with his hands. The boat came alongside of them and stopped. The captain came to the side where they were.

"What you damned swamp rats mean by stoppin' the boat?" shouted the captain.

"We want to know if'n you wants to buy a nice deer," said Pa.

"Throw up your line and we'll have a look," said the captain.

Pa threw the line up to a man, and he made it fast to the rail. They lowered two lines into the boat, and when Pa and Jeff had tied the lines to the deer's legs they pulled it up to the deck. The captain examined the deer.

"I'll give you twenty dollars for it," shouted the captain. "Send the small boy up your rope and I'll pay him."

Skeeter climbed the rope to the deck of the boat and went up to the captain to get the money. The captain had untied the boat rope behind Skeeter and held it in his hand. He motioned for two deck hands to come over to him.

"Throw this little bastard over the side," he said.

The two men grabbed Skeeter and heaved him over the side of the boat. The captain shouted down to Pa, "That'll teach you damned swamp rats not to stop the boat. Thanks for the deer." He laughed and signaled the wheelhouse for full speed ahead.

The churning water from the stern wheel of the boat sent Skeeter all the way to the bottom of the river. He felt his body hit the soft mud of the river bed. He thought he would never come up. His lungs were hurting, and he had taken in a lot of water. When he came up, he was thirty yards down the river. He fought madly to get upstream toward the boat. When Pa and Jeff saw him, they rowed to him and pulled him into the boat. He coughed water from his throat and lungs.

"You all right?" asked Pa.

"Yeah," said Skeeter.

"The Lord ain't goin' to stand fer sech as that much longer," said Pa. "One of these days he's goin' to take them boatmen slam off the river. I wish they was all in hell, myself."

They rowed on home and told Ma about what had happened. She almost cried when she learned that they had lost the deer for nothing.

"The Lord will take keer of them in His way," she said.

She had some of the fresh deer steaks cooking in the skillet, and the aroma soon took the thoughts of the boatmen from their minds. The men washed up while Ma finished the cooking. She put a heaping platter of steaks and a big bowl of gravy on the table. There was also a big pot of grits. The meat was so tender it fell to pieces as it was taken from the platter. Skeeter thought he had never eaten so much in his life. They all ate until every piece of the meat was gone.

They had to sit at the table for a while before they could get up.

"Well, I'll be derned," said Ma. "I got so mad when you told me about them boatmen that I clear forgot to tell you that we lost a hog after you all went back after that other deer."

"How you mean we done lost a hog?" asked Pa.

"Well, after me and Theresa had skinned that deer I walked down to the bayou to throw away hits feet when I seed the biggest 'gator I ever seed lyin' along the edge of the hog pen. He were jest lyin' there and waitin' fer one of them hogs to come close to the water. I grabbed a stick and throwed at him, but it didn't seem to bother him none. Then one of the hogs walked to the edge of the water, and he hit it with that big tail of hisen and knocked it in the water. Then he tore it all to pieces with them big jaws and didn't even eat it. He jest let it float off down the bayou. It near 'bout give me the creeps jest watchin' hit. That 'gator had the wildest look I ever seed in a critter's eyes, and the strange part about hit were that hit had whut looked like a big piece of metal stickin' out betwix its eyes."

"I bet it were the same critter whut knocked the fish box out'n the water that night," said Pa. "That critter must be either loco or downright mean, cause I never heerd of a 'gator pullin' tricks like that."

Skeeter felt his stomach almost turn sick. He knew that it was his fault that the hog had been killed, and it would be his fault for everything else the 'gator destroyed. He knew he should have listened to Jeff that night.

"I know whut it is, Pa," said Skeeter. "I seed that big 'gator in the swamp the night me and Jeff was frog giggin', and I planted a frog gig right betwix his eyes. He got away and broke the shaft, but he's still got the gig planted in his head. That 'gator's plumb lost his mind, Pa."

"If'n he's done gone crazy he mout kill ary thing that gits in his way, jest fer the love of killin'," said Pa.

"Don't you worry none about hit, Pa," said Skeeter. "Now that I got this rifle I'll git him fer shore afore the week is out."

"I guess we better call that old 'gator Steel Head till we gits him killed," said Pa. "That's shore a good name fer him with all the metal he's totin' aroun' in his brain."

"That air a good name at that, Pa," said Skeeter.

"Call him whut you wants," said Ma, "but you better git him afore he has all them hogs and us kilt, too. I'll be scared to go into the yard at night knowin' 'bout that critter bein' loose."

After everyone had gone to sleep, Skeeter lay awake thinking of ways he could track down and put an end to the life of Steel Head.

SEVEN

THE NEXT MORNING Jeff went with them to run the traps and lines. The traps were not cut, but the catch was small. Both traps did not yield over ten pounds of fish apiece, and the catch was also poor on the line. They had four cats, but they were all small ones. Pa rebaited the hooks, and they went home.

When they reached home, Jeff and Skeeter tacked the two deer hides to the side of the house to dry and cut the antlers from the head of the big buck. Then they threw the two heads into the bayou.

"Kin I have yore deer hide to sell, Skeeter?" asked Jeff. "I got to git up a little extra money fer somethin'. Pa's done said I could have hisen."

"You kin have mine if'n you'll go with me into the swamp tonight to see if'n I kin find that dern loco 'gator," said Skeeter.

"I shore ain't hankerin' to be in that swamp at night with that critter runnin' aroun' loose," he said, "but I'll do hit fer that hide."

"I'm goin' to take the rifle this time," said Skeeter, "so they ain't no use to be skeered."

"Jest the same I don't like hit," said Jeff.

"I think I'll go kill us a rabbit fer dinner," said Skeeter. "I been havin' a cravin' lately fer some good rabbit stew. Want to go with me, Jeff?"

"I'm still too sore from the fight and all that walkin' yesteddy to go huntin' anymore," said Jeff. "I'd ruther stay here and sit on the porch."

Skeeter picked up his gun and walked to the woods at the back of the clearing. He walked along kicking the bushes and trying to scare up a rabbit. A big cottontail jumped from a bush, and he shot it on the run.

"I believe I'll try the next un with the knife," he said out loud. He pulled the knife from his belt and changed the rifle to his left hand. When he kicked up the next rabbit, he sailed the knife straight into its side. "Guess I'm ready to tangle with old Steel Head now," he said. He walked back to the house, cleaned the rabbits, and took them in to Ma. She put them into a pot to parboil before making the stew.

After dinner, Pa, Jeff, and Skeeter were sitting on the front porch when they heard loud shouting and guns shooting on the river. They jumped to their feet startled.

"What in tarnation do you reckon that air?" said Pa. "Hit sounds like somebody's done took up a feud on the river."

Two boats whipped into the mouth of the bayou and started toward the house. They saw that it was the Hookers in their new boats. The old man was standing in the bow of the boat in the lead, and he looked like an old Indian chief leading his warriors. The Corey men ran down to the landing.

"Howdy, Abner," said the old man. "We's jest out tryin' our new boats. Don't you and yore boys want to go with us fer the ride?"

"I'd be powerful pleased to ride in them things," said Pa.

Theresa came to the back door and looked down at the landing. Sparky saw her and climbed out of the boat.

"If'n hit's jest the same to you, Pa," he said, "I'd like to stay here till you gits back from down the river."

"Now, you jest go on up there and git you some good sparkin' done," said the old man. "I knows jest how you feels. Evertime I see that girl, hit makes me wish I were forty years younger."

As Sparky walked to the house, Pa got into the boat with the old man, and Jeff and Skeeter got into the other one. When the boats reached the mouth of the bayou, the old man signaled them to stop.

"Pass the jugs around fust, and then we's going to have a race to Mill Town," he said. "Git both boats in the middle of the river, and when I fire my gun, take off."

The jugs were passed around, and everyone except Skeeter took a deep drink. Then they rowed the boats to the middle of the river and lined them up side by side. The old man stood in the bow and raised his gun in the air. When he pulled the trigger, they let out a loud yelp, and the boats were off with a jerk.

Skeeter had never been on anything moving so fast in his life. The boats were almost skimming the water. Each of the four oars touched the water at the same time, and each came out of the water at the same time. The old man stood in the bow of his boat and shouted wildly for more speed. He reloaded his gun and shot it into the air. It didn't seem to Skeeter that they had been on the river but a few minutes when Mill Town came in sight.

The boats were still running neck and neck when they passed the dock at the mill. The old man signaled them to boat their oars, and they let the boats coast until they lost some of their speed. Then they rowed back up the river and tied the boats to the docks.

"We mout as well git some sugar and some meal while we's down here," said the old man. "And when we gits through, we kin go by the saloon and watch that nigger play the joos harp a little. You boys bring a couple of jugs along. We mout want to wet our whistles afore we gits back to the boat."

They all got out of the boats and walked up the lane to the business street. Each one had his gun in his hand, and two of the boys carried a jug of whiskey. The old man went into a store and bought a hundred pounds of sugar and a hundred pounds of meal. Two of the boys put the sacks on their backs, and they crossed the street to the saloon. As they entered the door, the bartender came around and stopped them.

"You can't come in here and bring your own whiskey," he said. "That's agin the house rules."

"Hit 'pears to me we is already in," said the old man, "but if'n you wants to put us out, that's another thing."

He turned around and faced the boys. "Boys, this here varment says we can't come in here with our own whiskey. Don't you think hits might stuffy in here. They ought to be a little more air comin' in."

The bartender heard the click of nine gun hammers being cocked at one time. They raised their guns towards the roof and fired, and when the smoke cleared there could be seen nine holes blown in the roof.

"Do you think we could sit a spell now?" asked the old man.

"Anything you wants is on the house," said the bartender.

"Well, you owes us a dollar fer puttin' ventilation in this here place," said the old man.

The bartender pulled out a dollar bill and handed it to him.

"Now git that little nigger out here to dance and play that joos harp afore my trigger finger gits itchy and my aim gits bad."

The Negro came out, but he was nearly scared to death. His eyes were as big as buckets, and his hands shook so that he could hardly hold the harp.

"That little bugger shore air nervous," said the old man. "Git a water glass and let's give him a drink to kinda settle him down."

The bartender handed them a water glass, and Sun Up filled it to the brim with the white lightning whiskey. The old man motioned to the Negro to come over.

"Let's see how fast you kin kill this whiskey," he said.

"Boss man, I can't git that much of that stuff down," said the Negro.

Pa clicked the hammer of his gun, and the Negro took the glass and started drinking the whiskey. Water poured from his eyes, but he drank it to the last drop. He put the glass down and staggered around the room.

"Jest look at him," said the old man, "he's as drunk as a jaybird in a chinaberry tree. Now, give us a little music, boy."

The Negro's nervousness was now all gone, and he played his jew's harp and danced as he had never done before.

The jugs were passed many times, and they sat and watched for more than two hours. Finally the old man told them it was time to go, but before they left, he called the Negro over to him and gave him a dollar bill. The Negro thanked him profusely, and they left the saloon. The bartender sighed with relief.

Pa had not noticed that Jeff was not with them until they got back to the boats. Jeff came down the street and joined them on the dock. When they got into the boats and started up the river, they made better time than the Coreys could make coming down. It was not long before they reached the landing at the Corey house.

"Won't you all git out and come in?" asked Pa.

"We better git on up the river," said the old man. "We got a batch to run off at the still afore hit gits dark."

Sparky came out of the house and down to the boat landing. As Theresa stood on the stoop and watched him, he got into one of the boats.

"Hit's goin' to be full moon Satterday night," said the old man, "and we air plannin' on goin' in the woods and runnin' the foxes some. We goin' to go in jest a little below yore house, and we kin pick you up if'n you wants to go."

"I'd be much obliged to you if'n you did," said Pa.

The Hookers rowed down the bayou, and when they reached the river, the Coreys heard a shot and much yelling. They knew that another race was on.

Pa had had a little too much whiskey during the afternoon, so he went to bed as soon as supper was done. Ma and Theresa stayed in the kitchen to work on their new dresses. Jeff and Skeeter were in their room getting ready for the trip to the swamp. Both had knives on their belts, and Skeeter was putting shells for the rifle in his pocket.

"We goin' to carry a frog gig with us?" asked Jeff.

"Naw," said Skeeter. "Tain't no use to fool with them frogs if'n we's goin' to try to git that 'gator. He'll give us all the huntin' we has time to do."

They selected the biggest pine torch they could find and lit it on the hearth. When they got outside, Skeeter rubbed some of the stinking mosquito potion on his face. Jeff refused when he passed the bottle to him, and they walked down to the landing. Jeff got in the back of the skiff to pole, and Skeeter stood in the bow. He laid the rifle down and held the torch as they started toward the swamp.

They made several circles around the edge of the swamp but didn't see any signs of the alligator. Each time they made a circle they would go a little deeper into the swamp. They saw several small alligators and many big frogs, but still no sign of Steel Head.

"Let's go in a pretty fer piece and work our way back," said Skeeter. "I know that 'gator ain't gone to the hills. He's bound to be here somewheres."

"Well, you be kerful up there and keep them snakes out'n the skiff," said Jeff. "First one of them snakes you lets git in here I'm goin' to quit and go home."

Jeff poled the skiff straight towards the heart of the swamp. They went around trees and through vines and sometimes had to back up and turn around when they came to a dead end. The further in they got the thicker was the foliage.

"I jest ain't goin' no further, 'gator or no 'gator," said Jeff. "I don't believe a person could go all the way through this swamp unless he got down and crawled on his belly."

When Jeff turned the skiff around and started back, they could see only the distance ahead of them that the light covered. It was like being in a lighted ball with the outside painted black. They did not head straight back toward the bayou, but made long sweeping runs back and forth so they could cover much of the swamp. They saw many strange sights, but no signs of the big 'gator. As they were getting close to the edge of the swamp, Jeff stopped the skiff.

"Whut's that?" he asked.

They sat in silence for a few moments and then heard loud bellowing noises and water splashing somewhere in the darkness. Jeff poled in the direction of the sound. Skeeter picked up the rifle and cocked it.

"Now, go slow," said Skeeter, "cause if'n that's him, I shore don't want to come up on him all at once."

As they eased through the vines and trees, the sounds became louder. All at once the noise stopped, and they could hear a splashing going away from them. Jeff speeded up a little and Skeeter signaled for him to stop.

"Jest look at that," said Skeeter. "Have you ever seed sech a sight before?"

"Hit beats arything I ever seed," said Jeff.

There was a big bull 'gator about twelve feet long lying on a mudbank. He was torn and slashed, and his tail was nearly ripped from his body. The water was stained crimson with blood. They had never seen anything torn up so badly.

"That's shore the work of old Steel Head," said Skeeter.

"Wouldn't no critter in his right mind tear up one of his brother critters like that fer no reason at all. Let's see if'n we kin hear him."

They listened and heard a splashing not too far ahead of them. Jeff poled slowly in the direction of the sound, and then the sound stopped.

"He's stopped," said Skeeter. "He's lying up somewhere ahead of us, so go slow and keep yore eyes open."

As they poled slowly through the darkness, sweat was beginning to run down their faces. Skeeter's grip tightened on the rifle, and Jeff's hands shook a little as he pushed the pole. When they came into a group of big cypress knees, Jeff suddenly pushed the skiff sideways and started shouting wildly.

"There he is!" he shouted. "Right there in them cypress knees!" The 'gator was lying between two big knees and they had not been able to see him until they were right on him.

Skeeter wheeled around and aimed the rifle. The 'gator shot out of the knees like a bolt of lightning and went under the skiff. When his body hit the bottom of the skiff it knocked the skiff sideways. Skeeter fell off balance, and the gun fired into the water.

"Don't drop the torch!" shouted Jeff. "For gosh sake's don't drop the torch!" He was almost wild with fear.

Skeeter scrambled to his feet and held the torch above him as he hurriedly reloaded the rifle. The 'gator was lying right along the side of the skiff, popping his jaws madly. Skeeter took aim with the rifle. The 'gator hit the side of the skiff with his tail and knocked it several feet through the water. Jeff fell to the bottom of the skiff, and Skeeter had to grab the sides to keep from going into the water. He almost dropped the torch in the water, and the gun went off in the air. The 'gator came alongside of them and hit the skiff with his tail again, knocking it into the cypress knees. He bellowed loudly and went off through the darkness.

Skeeter and Jeff were lying in the bottom of the skiff, but they had not lost their light. Skeeter still had the torch in his hand. It was several minutes before either of them said anything. Jeff got up and pushed the skiff off the cypress knees.

"I wouldn't come in here again after that 'gator fer a thousand deer hides," he said. "A critter that could rip up a tough 'gator hide like that thing done wouldn't even need no teeth to tear me or you up."

Jeff poled the skiff out of the swamp as fast as he could. Skeeter didn't say anything for a long time.

"I'll git him afore I'm done," he finally said.

"Hit'll be more likely he gits you," said Jeff.

EIGHT

"DID YOU BOYS see that 'gator last night?" Pa asked.

"We seed him, Pa," said Skeeter, "but we didn't git him. He were too fast fer us last night."

"And that ain't the wust of hit," said Jeff. "I ain't goin' to see him no more if'n I kin help hit. That dern 'gator could snap a log in two with one whop. No, sir, I ain't goin' near that swamp at night agin fer nobody."

"I'll get him," said Skeeter. "You jest wait and see."

Ma was cooking the remaining eggs that Pa had bought, now that Jeff was fully recovered and could enjoy them. She fried some strips of salt pork and made a pot of grits. The food was steaming hot when they sat down to eat, and Pa took big helpings of everything because he was always especially hungry on a morning after he had been drinking white lightning.

The men got ready to go up the river. Pa was waiting for Jeff and Skeeter in the kitchen.

"If'n the ketch air as pore as hit were yesteddy we better stay up there and run them traps all day," said Pa, "so you

93

better throw us somethin' in a sack to eat if'n we don't come back. Won't be no use goin' to town tomorrow if'n we don't git some fish today. Hit wouldn't be wuth the trip down fer what we got now."

Ma fried a few slices of pork and made a small corn pone and put it in a sack. Pa took the food and they left the landing. After they had run the traps and line, Pa decided they had better stay on the river all day, because the catch had been poor again. They had taken only about fifty pounds of fish. If they ran the traps all day, they could get the fish out before the gar could get in and tear the netting, and they could get the cats off the trotline before a turtle had a chance to eat their bodies. They went from the traps to the line continuously, except for the time they took to eat their small dinner. Pa believed that their labor had been worth it, though, because they made a good catch during the day. They caught a hundred pounds of fish, and with what they had caught all week, he believed they would have a good load.

After supper, Jeff took down the deer hides and rolled them into a bundle to take to town and sell the next day. Skeeter was going to take the antlers to Uncle Jobe as a gift, for he always had to take the old Negro some kind of a present. Pa sat on the front porch for a while before going to bed. When the moon came over the cypress trees, it was as red as a big ball of fire. Pa went back into the kitchen where Ma and Theresa were working on their dresses.

"The moon air full tonight," he said, "so'es you better plant them seeds tomorrow while we air in town. They always does better if'n they's planted on the first day of full moon, 'specially the corn. And mix up some of that hog feed and give them pore hogs in the morning. The way they looked today, I don't believe they's goin' to last till killin' time."

"They'd do all right if'n you'd feed 'em once in a while," said Ma. "The pore things done grubbed all the roots out'n the ground."

"I jest plum forgit about feedin' 'em," said Pa. "I'll git ole Skeeter to give 'em somethin' ever day from now on."

Pa and the boys reached the boat docks at Mill Town by midmorning. They pulled the string of fish onto the dock. It was not nearly as heavy as it had been the week before, so Pa and Skeeter could handle it by themselves. They started to market with the fish, while Jeff went to sell his deer hides. Skeeter had the deer antlers with him. After Pa had been paid for the fish, they came out on the street.

"Kin I go see Uncle Jobe while you air gittin' the supplies?" asked Skeeter.

"I guess you kin," said Pa, "but don't be gone too long, and meet me back in front of the store."

Skeeter skipped happily down the lane to the Negro quarters. He found Uncle Jobe, as he always did, sitting on the porch of his house.

"Howdy, Uncle Jobe," said Skeeter.

"Well, dog if'n hit ain't Massah Skitter agin," he said. "Come on in and sot a spell."

Skeeter crossed the yard and sat on the front porch.

"I went deer huntin' the other day, and I done brought you some antlers. I killed him right by myself, too."

"Did you now, child?" asked Uncle Jobe. "I'm right proud uv you. And I sho' likes the gift you done brought me."

"Has you ever seed ary deer, Uncle Jobe?" asked Skeeter.

"Lawsy me, Massah Skitter, when I was a boy yore age there was so many deer thet they would come up and run with the cattle and hosses. At the plantation where I was brought up, I seed as many as fifty crossin' a field at one time, and we used to find one near 'bouts every day with his antlers caught in a fence. Sometimes when one of them big bucks would git caught, he'd fight so hard thet hit would break his neck."

"They ain't near 'bouts that many now, air they?" asked Skeeter.

"No, they ain't. They's been too many kilt jest fer the pleasure uv killin' 'em. They's still more then 'nough aroun', if'n everybody would jest git whut they need."

"We killed two," said Skeeter. "We took one home to eat and tried to sell the other one to the steamboat men. They throwed us a line and pulled the deer up on the deck, and when I went up the rope to git the pay, they throwed me in the river and made off with the deer."

"I knowed they was things like thet goin' on," said Uncle Jobe. "I kin feel hit in the air. They's trouble brewin' on this river with all the sin and them people treatin' you swamp folks like you was lower than the dogs. The Lord didn't make this river fer hit to be this way, and one of these days He's goin' to fix hit so'es them boats can't even go up the river. And they ain't gonna be no more deer or no other critters left fer folks to eat, and all the folks am goin' to have to go away."

"I shore hope nothin' like that don't ever happen," said Skeeter.

"These folks is sho' goin' to have to change their ways," said Uncle Jobe, "or somethin' air goin' to happen to 'em."

"I better be gittin' on back now," said Skeeter. "See you agin, Uncle Jobe."

When Skeeter reached the store, Pa was waiting for him, and they carried the supplies down to the boat and waited for Jeff to return. In a few minutes Jeff came back, and they started up the river for home. This Saturday had been a lot different from the last, and they were all secretly glad of it, especially Jeff.

When they reached home, they took the supplies into the kitchen and went to the front porch to sit. It was a good while before supper, and they had nothing to do.

"You boys goin' on the fox run tonight?" asked Pa.

"I don't keer nothin' 'bout goin'," said Jeff. "I had enough fer one week myself."

"You goin', Skeeter?" he asked.

"Shore," said Skeeter. "It'd take a broken leg to keep me from goin' with 'em."

They sat around and talked the rest of the afternoon, and Skeeter told them what Uncle Jobe had said about the river people and what was going to happen. Finally the sun went down, and they went in and ate supper. It was not long after they had finished when they heard the Hookers coming up the bayou. Pa and Skeeter went down to the landing and were waiting when the boats came in. The Hookers had four hounds tied in one boat.

"Git out and come in a spell afore we go," said Pa.

"I don't speck we got the time," said the old man. "The moon will be up by the time we gits down the river, and these old hounds air about to go crazy to git in them woods. They near 'bout jumped out'n the boat comin' down. You all ready to go, Abner?"

"Jest me and Skeeter here goin'," said Pa. "Jeff says he don't want to go this time. I think he's done gone to bed."

"Sparky here ain't goin' either," said the old man. "That boy's got the sickness mouty bad. Says he ruther stay here with Theresa than go on a good fox hunt. Never thought I'd see the day, but I guess I's jest too old to remember when I were a young buck."

Sparky got out of the boat, and Pa and Skeeter got in, and they started from the house. Theresa met Sparky on the back stoop, and they went out and sat on the front porch. Jeff was already asleep.

*   *   *

By the time the Hookers tied the boat up down the river, the moon was out, and it was nearly as bright as day. Sun Up took the dog chains and pulled the hounds up the bank. Two of the boys brought jugs of whiskey, and one brought a whole, dressed pig. They made their way, single file, through the thick brush and vines and kept going until they reached a pine thicket in the big woods. They raked a big circle clean of pine straw and started piling up wood for a fire. When they had brought enough wood to burn all night and had a big blaze going, they cleaned another circle and started a smaller fire to one side. The old man cut two forked sticks, which he put in the ground on each side of the fire. Then he cut a straight one, sharpened it, and ran it through the whole length of the pig. He cut a small stick and tied to the end of the long one going through the pig so it would be easy to turn while the pig was roasting. Then he put the pig over the small fire and assigned Skeeter the task of keeping it turned.

"Well, you kin turn 'em loose now, Sun Up," said the old man.

Sun Up released the chains from the collars, and the hounds bounded off through the woods. They let out a low, wailing yelp as they ran, and the men gathered around the fire, waiting for the dogs to strike.

"Open up a jug and let's all have a little snort," said the old man. "They ain't nothin' like a good drink uv whiskey out in the woods at night." The jug was passed around, and everyone took a good drink. Pa and the old man took a second drink before they put the stopper back.

"When you goin' to teach that boy there to take a good drink, Abner?" asked the old man.

"He says hit burns his belly too bad, and he don't keer fer hit," said Pa.

"Well, I guess we'd be better of if'n we were like that, but I shore do enjoy a good drink uv whiskey."

When they heard the hounds let out a shrill yelp far in the distance, they knew that they had struck the trail of a fox.

"Jest listen to that music," said the old man. "They ain't nothin' like bein' in the woods at night and listenin' to the hounds run, and havin' plenty of good whiskey to drink, and a pig roastin' over a fire, and good friends about you."

"I likes hit mighty fine, too," said Pa. "I'm right pleased you axed me to come."

Skeeter was sitting on the ground turning the pig over the blaze. "Ain't we goin' to follow them dogs since they has struck that fox?" he asked.

"Tain't no use to do that, Son," said the old man. "They'll bring him right back around to here if'n they don't ketch him fust."

They could hear the yelping of the dogs as they made a wide circle around them. The jug was passed again, and everyone was beginning to feel in a good mood. The boys sang songs while Pa and the old man talked. After a while the sound of the hounds became louder, and the men could tell that they were coming straight back to where they had started.

"They ain't goin' to ketch that one," said the old man. "Go git him."

Two of the boys picked up their guns and walked off toward the sound of the hounds. In a few minutes a gun was fired, and they walked back to the fire carrying a red fox, which they hung by the tail in a tree. The dogs came in, sniffed the fox for a few minutes, and were gone again. The jug was passed to toast the first kill. In a few minutes, the dogs struck again, but this time they caught the fox and brought him back. He was hung up beside the other one, and the dogs were off again.

By midnight three jugs were gone, and everybody was getting pretty drunk. They didn't pay as much attention to the dogs. Conversation was flowing freely, and the boys were beginning to play a little rough.

"Let's have a bear rassel," shouted Full Moon. "Me and Sun Down, High Noon and Low Twelve will take on the rest of you."

They all stripped off their clothes and formed in two straight lines facing each other. When Pa shouted "go," they immediately became a mass of tangled flesh and bones. They threw each other on the ground and piled on, and rolled all over the thicket. Skeeter thought they were going to kill each other. The fight went on for a half hour, and finally the old man shouted for them to stop. He told them that it was a draw, so they took a big drink from the jug and put on their clothes.

By this time the pig was roasted to a golden brown, so the old man removed it from the fire and placed it beside a huge sack of corn pone and baked potatoes that his wife had prepared for the hunt. Each man came by and cut himself a big chunk of the meat, and then came back for seconds. They ate until there was not a piece of flesh left on the bones. As they washed it down with another drink of whiskey, the old man signaled for the boys to be quiet.

"Listen at that," he said. "That ain't no fox them dogs has got. They got a wildcat treed out there."

The dogs were yelping wildly and in a much higher pitch than they had been doing.

"Let's go git him," said the old man.

They picked up their guns and went off toward the dogs. When they reached them, the dogs were in a circle around a small sweetgum tree. They could see a big wildcat in its top, so several of the boys raised their guns to shoot.

"Don't shoot!" cried the old man. "Let's make a good fight out'n hit. A couple of you boys go over there and shake him out fer the dogs, but be shore and git out'n the way in a hurry, cause that critter kin tear the fool out'n you."

Two of the boys went over and shook the tree until the cat fell to the ground, and then ran as fast as they could. The dogs were on the cat immediately, and then the cat was on the dogs. The air was filled with the screeching and yelping of the fight. The dogs were trying to get their teeth on the cat's throat, and the cat was slashing long gashes in their flesh with its claws. For a few minutes it looked like the cat was going to win, but one of the dogs got it behind the neck with its teeth and the fight was soon ended. The dogs tore the cat to pieces, and then they ate its flesh.

"You better put the chains on them hounds now," said the old man. "Since they's tasted that wildcat meat we'd never git 'em out of the woods."

Sun Up chained the dogs, and they went back to the fire. When they finished the last jug of whiskey, they put out the fire. The dawn was just breaking when they reached the boat and started up the river. They were still so drunk when they reached the Corey house that they forgot about Sparky and went on and left him. Pa staggered into the house and fell onto the bed. Sparky was in the bed with Jeff, so Skeeter went out on the porch and went to sleep. He decided that he had had enough fox hunting to last him a long time.

NINE

IT WAS LATE that afternoon when the Hookers came back after Sparky, and only four of them came. Sparky said good-by to Theresa and left. Pa was still asleep, but Skeeter had just got up and gone to the back of the house to wash the sleep from his eyes. He went into the back yard to see if the foxes were still where he had left them. The Hookers had given them to him, and he had brought them home to give the hides to Jeff. He called Jeff to the back yard.

"We better skin these foxes afore they spoil," he said. "I thought they mout be worth somethin', so you kin take 'em to town the next time you go, and see."

They skinned the foxes, and Jeff tacked the hides to the side of the house, and they played mumble peg until darkness fell.

The next week did not bring as much excitement as the previous one had. They spent most of their time running the traps and the line. Three days they had to stay on the river all day to make a good catch, and one day they found the trap torn again. Skeeter spent all the spare time he could get killing snakes, so Jeff could have the skins to get the extra money he had secretly said he needed.

Jeff never mentioned what he wanted the money for, and Skeeter never asked, for they never pried into each other's private affairs.

By the end of the week they had made a good enough catch to make the trip to Mill Town. After they had tied up to the dock, Pa and Skeeter took the fish to the market, while Jeff went to sell the fox hides and the snakeskins. Skeeter went to see Uncle Jobe, while Pa bought the supplies, and then they met in front of the store and took the supplies down to the boat. Jeff was not there so they sat down to wait. They waited a long time, and Jeff still did not return. A small Negro boy came on the dock and walked up to Pa and Skeeter.

"Yore name Corey?" he asked.

"Hit shore air," said Pa. "Whut you got on yore mind?"

"This air fer you," said the Negro. He handed Pa a piece of paper and turned around and ran from the dock.

Pa turned it over and over and looked at it from all angles. Neither he nor Skeeter could read.

"Wonder whut this air," said Pa. "Hit's got writin' on hit. Don't know who'd be sendin' me some writin'."

"Why don't you keep hit till Jeff gits back?" said Skeeter. "He kin read a little bit."

"We'll jest do that," said Pa, "and if'n he can't read hit, we'll take hit home fer Theresa to read."

They waited a long time, and still Jeff didn't return. They heard the steamboat coming up the river, and they walked to the end of the dock to watch it pass. When it reached the big dock down the river at the mill, there was a white flag hoisted on a post of the dock, so the boat pulled in and tied up.

"Wonder whut the boat's stoppin' fer," said Pa. "They don't load no lumber on Satterday afternoon."

"Hit beats me, Pa," said Skeeter.

They could see two people walk up the plank and board the boat. Then the plank was pulled in, the lines cast off, and the boat came on up the river and passed out of view.

"Jest a couple of people gittin' on," said Pa. "Wonder who they was? Too fer off to see who they was."

They waited until late afternoon and still Jeff had not come back. Pa was beginning to get worried about him.

"Can't understand hit," said Pa, "I ain't never knowed that boy to stay off this long withouts him telling me somethin'."

"Maybe that note's from him, Pa," said Skeeter. "Why don't we go and git Mr. Blanch to read hit to us."

"That sounds like a right good idea, Skeeter. Don't know why I hadn't thought of that afore now."

They walked up the lane to the fish market and went in the back entrance. Mr. Blanch did not have any customers in the market, so he came back to meet them.

"Don't tell me you've caught some more fish already, Abner," he laughed.

"Tain't that this time, Mr. Blanch. I was jest wonderin' if'n you would do me a favor."

"Why sure, if I can I'll be glad to."

"I got a note here a nigger brought me down to the docks, and I left my specks at home, so I can't read hit. Skeeter here ain't never had a chance to git no schoolin', so we was wonderin' if'n you would read hit fer us."

Pa handed the note to Mr. Blanch, and he turned it over and looked at it for a long time. It was written in a very poor hand, so it took him a long time to make out the words. Finally he turned to Pa and started reading:

DEAR PA,

I don't know how you air goin to feel when you reads this but I hope you don't feels too bad to me. Me and Clarise is leavin on the boat to git married and live up the river at Monticello. I has been savin up fer this since I got beat up and she has a little money too. The swamp woudn't be no place fer her to live with her used to the town and if'n we stayed aroun here hit would jest mean trouble fer all of us. As soon as we gits settle and has time we will write you at the post office at Mill Town and let you know how we are and everythin. Tell Skeeter I thank him fer helpin me git the money and tell Ma and Theresa goodby. You all take ker of yoreself and we'll be thinkin abouts you.

Yore son,
JEFF

Mr. Blanch handed the note back to Pa, and nobody said anything for a long time. Pa wiped a little mist from his eyes with his dirty hands. Skeeter just stood with his hands behind him.

"I never thought the boy would go so fer as that," said Pa, "but I guess he's got his own life to look out to."

They turned around and started out the back door. "Thank ye fer yore trouble, Mr. Blanch," said Pa. Mr. Blanch nodded his head.

They went back to the boat and rowed up the river in silence. It was dark when they reached the house. Ma and Theresa met them at the landing.

"Whut's done kept you so long?" asked Ma. "And where's Jeff?"

Pa didn't say a word but walked in the house with them following. He handed the note to Theresa and she read it to Ma. Ma sat at the table and buried her face in her hands for a long time. Finally she got up to get the supper.

"I knowed hit was goin' to come to that," she said, "and Jeff were right. The swamp wouldn't be no place fer them."

They ate their supper in silence, and the food did not taste good to any of them. Pa knew that the work would be harder now that Jeff was gone, and soon he would be losing Theresa. Skeeter was thinking of having to do his and Jeff's part of the work and how he wouldn't have as much time from now on to wander by himself in the swamp. Ma was just sick at losing her first-born son.

They went to bed, and the bed didn't feel the same to Skeeter without Jeff in it with him. He lay awake late into the night and could hear his mother crying in the next room. He didn't understand this part of life.

TEN

PA AND SKEETER went about the work and the fishing as best they could by themselves. It was a little harder running the traps and the line, without Jeff to help Skeeter row so Pa would be free to do the work, and it took them longer than it had before. The sun continued hotter, the rains were further apart, and it was as hot at night as it was in the day. The river dropped a little each day, and the further it dropped, the worse became the gar and turtle. Some weeks they had to stay on the river all day every day, and some weeks they didn't go to Mill Town because they did not have enough fish. They had to carry water in buckets from the bayou to the garden to water it, because the plants were almost fully grown.

It took the steamboats twice the length of time to make the trip up the river in the summer as it did at any other time of year. When the river was low, they had to creep along and take soundings every few feet, to keep from running on bars. The boats did not come by as often, because they could not pass each other on the river when it was low.

Some months during the summer only two boats ran the river. One would have to make the trip all the way up and wait for the other one to get there, before it could start back down.

One day Pa and Skeeter were working their traps at West Cut when they heard a steamboat coming up the river. West Cut was one of the most dangerous curves on the river during low water, and the boat was creeping along. They stopped their work to watch it make the turn. All the passengers were standing around the rails watching. When the boat passed the curve, it gathered speed to run over a bar; it hit the bar, and the jar turned the bow to the left, and the boat left the channel. It ran into a mudbank and tilted to one side. The engineer gave it full speed astern, and the paddle wheels sent tons of muddy water rising under the boat and onto the bank, but the boat did not move. It was stuck too tight to pull itself off. Pa and Skeeter rowed up to the side of the boat, and the captain came to the rail.

"I'll give you a dollar to help us get off this mudbank," he yelled.

"Give us the dollar fust," said Pa.

The captain cursed and threw a wadded dollar bill down to Pa. He unfolded it, looked at it, and put it in his pocket.

"Now, what you want us to do?" asked Pa.

"Row around to the stern and we'll lower an anchor down into your boat. You row back down the river until the line gets tight and then drop the anchor and get out of the way. We'll do the rest."

Pa and Skeeter rowed their boat to the stern and the anchor was lowered to them. They drifted back down the river until the line attached to the anchor became tight and then dropped it over the side. The men on the steamboat wrapped the line around the drum of a steam winch and took up the slack. Pa and Skeeter rowed over to the bank to watch. As the slack was taken out of the line, the anchor dug deeper into the mud at the bottom of the river. They intended to take up the line and pull the boat back to the anchor, and off the mudbank. As the line became tighter the boat moved a few feet and stopped. The engineer gave it full astern, and the men on the stern tightened with the winch. The line broke in the middle and sent a fine spray of manila hemp all over the river. The captain cursed and motioned for Pa and Skeeter to come back, so they rowed back to the boat.

"We can't get it off," said the captain, "and it'll be almost a week before they can send another boat up here to pull us off. I've got a lot of passengers on here and we couldn't bring much meat because of the heat, so I'll pay you to kill me a deer."

"Will you pay us afore you gits the deer on the boat?" asked Pa.

"Yes, damn you!" shouted the captain. "I'll pay you before we get the deer on the boat! And we'll buy some fish right now if you have any!"

The captain bought all the fish Pa and Skeeter had with them, and they rowed back down the river towards home. The next morning they were in the woods before sunup, and in an hour had killed a big buck. They bled him and skinned him on the bank of the river and loaded him in the boat. Skeeter cut off the antlers and threw the head in the river. They rowed back to West Cut, and the captain gave them twenty-five dollars for the buck, before they pulled it up to the deck. They sold them more deer before the other boat came, but what little fish they caught they had to take home to eat themselves. By the end of the week they did not have a single fish to take to Mill Town to sell, but they had the money to buy their supplies with.

Pa spent every bit of the money for food supplies, and Skeeter traded the deer hides for shot for his rifle. Pa knew that the fishing would become worse, and he wanted to have as much food as possible in store to tide them over.

As the days got hotter and the river dropped, the fishing became worse, and finally it was all Pa and Skeeter could do to stay on the river all day every day just to catch enough for the family to eat. The food supplies were getting shorter, and Ma would have to boil the same coffee for a week at a time. The traps would be torn nearly every day, and the turtles would eat the cat almost as soon as they would get on the line. The gars ate the bait so fast that it took more and more shot to kill squirrels and rabbits to keep the bait supply up. One day they came back home with both traps in the boat. Pa walked in the kitchen where Ma was and sat down.

"Tain't no use foolin' ourselves no longer," he said. "We can't make hit here with the fishin' like hit air now. They ain't even goin' to be meal to cook fish with soon, and I done et so much fish that my belly feels like a fish box."

"Whut you plannin' on doin'?" asked Ma.

"I was thinkin' 'bout goin' down to Mill Town and workin' at the mill till things gits better," he said. "We kin set the traps and the line at the mouth of the bayou here, and hit'll be easy fer Skeeter to run them. And they ought to be enough in the garden fer you to make out on. Skeeter kin come to town once every week, and I kin take my earnings and send the supplies back up by him."

"Now, you know Skeeter can't row that boat up the river by hisself."

"No, but I kin make him a paddle and he kin come in the skiff. The river ain't swift now, and he could make hit in that light skiff. I was goin' to take the boat with me."

Skeeter was sitting outside listening to the talk. He liked the idea of Pa being away for a while, for then he could have more time to himself, and could hunt old Steel Head again. He had not looked for the big 'gator since the night he and Jeff went into the swamp.

"But won't hit cost you as much as you make jest to stay in Mill Town?" asked Ma.

"I kin stay with that nigger friend of Skeeter's fer nothin'," said Pa, "and I kin eat light and save enough fer supplies. They was payin' fifteen cents an hour last week."

"Well, I guess hit beats stayin' here and starvin'. I hates to be left in this swamp with nobody but Skeeter and Theresa around, but I guess you better go. When you plannin' on leavin'?"

"Jest as soon as I kin git my few clothes together and git in the boat."

Pa went into his room and tied his belongings into a little bundle and came back to the kitchen. Skeeter was sitting on the floor.

"You go back up the river and take up that trotline and set hit down at the mouth of the bayou," he said. "And set them traps in the bayou. When the wood gits low, go over to the woods and git some more, but you be shore and be careful. Them critter over there gits mean this time of year. You do what yore Ma tells you, and look out fer them. If'n they's trouble, come down in the skiff and tell me."

Pa picked up the bundle and walked down to the landing with the rest of the family following him. He told them all good-by, got into the boat and shoved off down the bayou. When he reached the river, he stood up and waved back to them. Then he was gone from sight.

"He done went right off and forgot to make you that paddle," said Ma.

"Don't matter," said Skeeter, "I'll make hit myself."

Skeeter spent the rest of the morning making himself a paddle. When dinner was done, Ma called him to the house. Dinner didn't taste the same with only the three of them to eat, and he didn't feel quite as happy as he first had with the thought of being alone.

After dinner, he went up the river and moved the line to the mouth of the bayou and then came home to mend the traps. He took them to the front porch, and Theresa came out to help him. They sat in the hot sun, and Skeeter wanted to go to sleep. The heat felt good to him and seemed to draw all the energy from his body. In a few minutes his eyes closed, and Theresa went on with the mending.

He was awakened by loud shouting on the bayou. He looked up and saw the boats of the Hookers coming towards the house. Ma and Theresa were already down at the landing. He jumped up and ran down to meet them, but the boats had touched the bank when he got there.

"Howdy, Glesa," said the old man. "Where's Abner?"

"He went down to Mill Town this mornin' to git a job at the mill," she said. "The fishin' were gittin' so bad that our rations was gettin' mouty short. He's jest goin' to stay till the fishin' gits better."

"Well, I hates to hear that," said the old man. "Hits mighty bad when a family gits broke up cause of rations. If'n we had of knowed hit, we could have helped you out."

"I shore appreciate you sayin' that, but I know he'd ruther have hit this way. Abner never was much to ask fer help."

"I guess hits best fer a man to feel that way. Ever man feels like he'd best look after his family by hisself."

Theresa and Sparky were looking at each other and had not heard a word of the conversation. When they were together, they were not aware of anyone in the world but themselves.

"We were jest on our way to Mill Town and thought we would stop by and speak," said the old man. "You may as well git on out, Sparky, afore you has to ask me kin you stay."

Sparky got out of the boat, and the Hookers continued their trip to Mill Town. Ma went into the house to work on her dress, and Skeeter returned to the porch to finish mending the trap. Sparky and Theresa walked to the woods at the back of the clearing and sat down under a magnolia tree.

The tree was in full bloom, so Sparky climbed a limb and got Theresa one of the giant flowers. He put it in the side of her long red hair, and it was beautiful against its silky background.

"I wish we had a big cypress tree down here like you have," she said. "None of ours are near 'bouts that tall, and I think that tree is the purtiest thing on the river."

"I think you are the purtiest thing on the river," said Sparky.

Theresa blushed, and he took her in his arms and kissed her. He held her for a long time without speaking.

"When you think yore folks air goin' to let us git married?" he asked.

"I don't know," she said, "I ain't asked them. With things bein' so hard on us as they has been lately, I been ashamed to mention hit. I better stay around and help till things gits better."

"I guess that air the right thing to do," he said, "but I wish the time would hurry and come. I hates fer us to be apart so much."

"I hates hit, too, but maybe it won't be too long."

They sat for a long time talking and then got up and went back to the house. Theresa showed him the new dress she was making, and he told her that she would have to wear it when they went to the Christmas frolic at Mill Town together. Theresa thrilled at the thought of the frolic, for she had heard of it but never had been. She had never gone to any kind of a frolic in her life, for she had never known anything but work on a farm and the life in the swamp.

"You really goin' to take me to the frolic?" she asked.

"Shore, I am. And after we's married I'll take you ever year, and you'll have a new dress ever time to show them folks you air the best-lookin' woman on the river."

Theresa had never been called a woman before, and the word excited her. The thought of going to the frolic every year made her feel good, and she was so happy she thought she would cry. It made her sad when she heard the Hookers' boats come back to the landing. They walked down to meet them.

"Jest look at that," cried the old man. "Dog if'n that flower in that red hair don't make that gal look like some kind of a princess. I gets butterflies in my belly ever time I looks at her."

Theresa blushed and thanked him for the compliment.

"I seed Abner while we was there, Glesa," he said, "and he said to tell you he got the job all right, and air stayin' with Uncle Jobe, whoever that air. I didn't know you all had kinfolks down there."

"Hit ain't really kinfolks," said Ma, "hits jest a friend of Skeeter's." Ma didn't tell him it was an old Negro.

"He also said to tell Skeeter hit wouldn't be no use to come to town this week, to wait and come next Satterday. And he sent you this bag uv meal."

He handed the bag of meal to Ma, and even though she knew that Pa had not sent it, she took it. She knew that the old man had bought it himself, because Pa didn't have any money when he left.

"How about us comin' down and gittin' you folks early Sunday mornin' and you spendin' the day with us?" asked the old man. "We'd be mouty pleased to have you, and Bertha is cuttin' a fit to see that gal again."

"We'd be mighty pleased to," said Ma.

They waved good-by as the Hookers left and then went back to the house. Skeeter loaded the traps into the skiff and left to set them in the mouth of the bayou. When he finished, he came back and ate supper. Ma and Theresa worked on their dresses, and Skeeter cleaned his rifle. They all stayed up later than usual before going to bed. It was the first time Skeeter had ever spent a night without Pa, and it felt strange to him.

*   *   *

When Skeeter ran the line the next morning, there wasn't a fish on it, but he made a good catch in the traps. He knew that it was just that the fish were not used to the traps being there, and that the catch would not be as good the next time. It seemed that during low water the fish knew where the traps were, and would avoid them. But he was proud that he had made one good catch. It would make him feel big when he went to town next week and had fish to sell. He went back to the landing and put the fish into the fish box. The next morning when he went to the traps they were both torn up beyond repair, and new netting would have to be bought for both of them before they could be used again. He took them home and put them under the house.

It was early Sunday morning when the Hookers came for the Coreys. The old man had not come himself, but had sent four of the boys for them. He was waiting at the landing when they reached the Hooker place. He greeted them and they all went to the house together. The old woman met them at the door.

"Come on in, Glesa," she said, "I shore am proud to see you again. And there's that purty gal with you."

The old woman put her arm around Theresa and kissed her on the cheek. Sparky had not been in the boat that brought them, and Theresa looked around for him. In a few minutes he came in, and they went out to sit on the porch. Skeeter went down to the still, and the old folks sat in the front room to talk.

"I shore hated to hear 'bout Abner havin' to go off and work at the mill," said the old woman. "Hit's a shame when a thing like that happens to a woman. A woman jest naturally needs a man aroun' the house."

"I don't like hit a bit," said Ma, "but hit 'pears sometimes that the Lord jest don't want things to go too smooth fer a body. Seems like He wants to mix in a little of the bad with the good, so a person will appreciate the good more when he has hit."

"Well, I never thought about hit like that afore," said the old woman, "but I believe you is dead right. When things is too good, folks gits to takin' it fer granted, and then they don't 'speck nothin' no less. And when things gits bad, they don't know whut to do, and runs around like a bunch of lost hounds. I see now whut the Lord means when He gives folks a sort of a bad time."

"I believe if'n the Lord took some of them town folks and drapped them down on this riverbank like He did us, they'd starve to death afore they got their bearin's," said Ma.

"I 'spect you air right," said the old woman. "I 'spect you air right."

The two women went to the kitchen to prepare the dinner, and when it was done they called the boys in from the still. It was a big dinner, and after it was finished, the boys all went back to the still to sleep. When the dishes were done, the two women and the old man went to the front porch to sit and talk. Sparky and Theresa were walking towards the trail that led to the big cypress tree.

"Now jest look at that," said the old man. "Them two kids air goin' down to that big tree. Some days Sparky goes down there and jest sits fer hours by hisself. They must have some kind uv secret down there."

"Theresa talks about hit a lot, too," said Ma.

"I think when they gits married I'll build them a house down there so'es they kin spend all their time there," said the old man.

The old folks sat on the porch and talked for many hours, and it was late in the afternoon when Ma said they had better go. The old man gave them a side of salt pork and several jars of beans before they left. He told Ma that the boys would call for them next Sunday, and they would have another good visit. It was dark when the Coreys reached home and said good-by to the Hooker boys.

Sparky had made the trip back down with them, and Theresa hated to see him leave. They took the things the Hookers had given them into the kitchen, and Ma fixed some supper.

"Them Hookers air mouty good neighbors to have," she said. "We's lucky to have them aroun'."

"We shore air," said Theresa, but she meant it in a different way.

ELEVEN

THE WORK WAS EASY for Skeeter the next week without the traps to run. He had not told Ma about the good catch he had made the first night the traps were set in the bayou because he wanted to have fish to take to town Saturday. If they ate the fish, there would be no money to buy new netting for the traps. He saved what few fish he caught on the trotline to go with the others and kept Ma pleased by providing meat for the table by killing game. Now that the garden was grown, there was no danger of starving, but they had to have meat.

Ma had made Skeeter a pair of shorts from an old pair of overalls that he had outgrown, and they were the only clothes he wore. His skin was as brown and as tough as a piece of leather, and his hair was bleached yellow by the hot summer sun. He would spend long hours lying in the bottom of the skiff, drifting on the bayou, and when his skin became hot, he would slip off the shorts and dive into the cool water. He liked to swim naked in the cool black water of the bayou and lie among the marsh grass and water lilies. Sometimes he would chase a snake from a log or try to slip up on an unsuspecting crane.

He also spent many hours of the afternoons in the swamp, always on the watch for Steel Head. He found bodies of several small 'gators torn to shreds and knew that Steel Head was still in the swamp, but he could not find the big 'gator. He knew that his best chance to find him was at night, but he could not hunt him without Jeff to pole for him while he held the torch. But he never gave up the idea of killing the 'gator. He seemed to know that they would meet again in combat, and the next time was his turn to win.

Now each day he had a new task—watering the garden. He carried many buckets of water from the bayou and poured on the thirsty plants. The marsh grass and the trees and bushes were parched red from the lack of rain, and without the water the garden would dry in a few days. When he finished, he went back to the house and into the kitchen where Ma and Theresa were sweating from the heat.

"Let's go nigger fishin' today, Ma," he said. "The bream air bedded up now, and I know where they's a bunch of good beds. I'll dig the worms if'n you and Theresa wants to go with me."

"That's a right good idea, Skeeter," said Ma. "Hit would do us good to git out'n this hot house fer a change. And I'd like to have a good mess of them bream fried good and crisp."

Skeeter went to the back of the clearing to dig the worms, while Ma and Theresa finished their housework. When he returned, he took three slender cane poles from under the house and rigged them for bream fishing. He put on long lines and small hooks and quills he had made from the stems of marsh grass. Ma made a small lunch to take with them, and she and Theresa put on their sunbonnets and came down to the landing. Skeeter already had the poles and worms in the skiff.

"I got some of them long red worms," he said, "and a few grasshoppers. Them red worms is the best bait they air. We ought to ketch a barrelful. I brought a fish string with me."

"Well, I jest hope we ketch 'nough to make the skillet smell," said Ma.

"You better sit in the middle, Ma, so'es the skiff won't sink," said Skeeter.

"Why, you little varment," she said, laughing.

They got into the skiff, and Skeeter poled up the bayou in the direction of the swamp. When they reached the point where the bayou merged with the swamp, Skeeter turned the skiff to go along the south side. The edges of the swamp were not thick with vegetation as it was further in, so Ma and Theresa were not afraid to go there. Tall, towering cypress trees and cypress knees rose out of the water, and little islands of marsh grass were scattered about. The water was very still and clear, but the dead leaves and trash on the bottom made it look black. Tall white cranes and gray cranes and water turkeys stood around the islands of marsh grass pecking at the crawfish and minnows. Ducks floated lazily on the water, and turtles were sunning themselves on logs.

Skeeter stopped the skiff several yards out from a clump of cypress knees. There was a spot on the bottom, close to the knees, that was white instead of black, and that was where the bream had made their bed. He unrolled the lines, set the quills, and strung a worm on each of the hooks. Then he handed one to Ma and Theresa.

"You jest as well wait a minute afore you throw in," he said. "Them bream scare easy and hit'll be a little bit afore they comes back to the bed. And don't make no noise if'n you kin help hit."

They sat very still and quiet for a few minutes and then threw the lines over the bed. As soon as the baits sank to the bottom they shot off towards the knees and the thin cane poles bent double. They were catching the bream as fast as their baits hit the water. Some of the fish would weigh three pounds, and none were smaller than both Skeeter's hands put together. Bream that size were not found anywhere but in the swamp, as the ones in the creeks and bayou were much smaller.

A minnow swam lazily by the side of the skiff, and Skeeter scooped it up with his hands. He cut the small hook from his line and put on a larger one, and pulled the quill down until it was only a foot from the hook. Then he hooked the minnow through the tail and threw it away from the bream bed. The minnow pulled the quill around the top of the water for a few seconds and then went under with a splash of water. The end of the cane pole popped the water madly, and Skeeter thought it would break. He made no attempt to pull the fish in, but just let it fight with the line and the pole. Ma and Theresa stopped fishing to watch. The fish would take Skeeter's line in wide circles around the skiff and would come towards the skiff and then go the other way. Skeeter held the line tight but allowed the pole to play as much as it would. The fish tried to take the line into the cypress knees, but Skeeter would hold it back. The fight went on for a half hour, and finally the fish began to give up. Skeeter pulled it to the side of the skiff, grabbed the line and yanked it into the skiff. It was a bass that would weigh at least ten pounds.

His arms were tired from the fight, so he did not fish any more. He sat and watched Ma and Theresa catch the big bream until the bait was gone, and then they started home.

He poled the skiff close to the grass islands so he could watch the big cranes fly away, and he steered close to logs and knocked turtles into the water with his pole. He took them around big trees and through groups of cypress knees so he could show Ma and Theresa more beds that the bream had made and places where the 'gators made their dens.

They watched a snake stalk a small frog, then swallow it whole, and Theresa almost cried when she saw it. She wanted Skeeter to kill the snake and get the frog from its stomach, but he just laughed and went on.

Coming out of the swamp they passed a large mudbank, and Skeeter saw a moccasin curled in the muck. He poled the back of the skiff to the bank and stepped out. "I'm goin' to show you how to ketch that varment," he said.

"You better git back in here and leave that thing alone," said Ma. "You jest askin' fer trouble. Whut you think we'd do if'n that thing bit you, and us up here in this swamp?"

"He ain't goin' to," he said.

He broke a reed from a piece of grass, and holding it in his left hand, eased over to the snake. When he was close enough, he waved the reed in front of the snake. It raised up from the coil and held its head high for a few seconds, its tongue darting back and forth from its mouth, then it struck at the reed. Skeeter's right hand shot out as quick as a flash and grabbed the snake just behind the head. Ma and Theresa were terrified as they watched. He threw the reed down and transferred the snake to his left hand. It wrapped its body around his arm, and he started back to the skiff.

"Don't you dare bring that thing in this skiff!" shouted Ma.

"I were jest goin' to let you look at him," said Skeeter.

"I don't want to look at him!" said Ma. "If'n that's whut you been doin' whiles you is always up here in this swamp, I don't see how you has lived to be as old as you are."

"You want to see his brains pop out?" asked Skeeter.

"I don't keer whut you do with him, jest so long as you don't bring him in this skiff," said Ma.

He unwrapped the snake's body from his arm, took the end of it with his right hand, swung both arms back to the left, let go the head, slung it out with his right hand and jerked it back. The snake popped like a whip, and its brains

hit the water ten feet away. Skeeter brought the limp body
back to the skiff with him.

"I'll trade this fer some likker sticks Satterday," he said.

"Well, you shore better not ever do that again with me
around," said Ma. "That dern near scared me to death, and
jest look at Theresa shakin'. We don't want to see you git
yoreself kilt." He threw the limp body into the skiff and
poled back to the landing.

They all helped clean the fish, and Ma and Theresa carried them to the house. They had much more than they
could eat, so Skeeter saved the smaller bream to put on his
trotline. He knew that the big cat liked bream better than
anything he could put on the hooks, but the turtle and gar
liked them too, so he would have to run the line that night
if he expected to catch a big cat. He put them in a bucket of
water to keep. When he finished, he pulled off his clothes
and swam in the water of the bayou. He baited the hooks
just before dark and returned to the house.

Ma was frying the fish they had caught, and it smelled a
lot better to him than the smell of catfish. He had eaten so
much catfish that he didn't get any joy out of it any longer,
but he liked the sweet crisp taste of the bream and bass.
They were not full of muddy water as the cats were. Ma
fried them to a crisp, golden brown and put them on the
table, and Skeeter thought of Pa and Jeff as he ate, because
he knew that they both liked the bream as well as he did.

Skeeter lay awake until about midnight, then got up and
went down to the landing to go run the trotline. He got the
gaff from under the house and paddled down the bayou. The
water where the line was set was too deep to use the pole.
The moon was out, and it cast a pale silver glow over the
flats of marsh grass. The night air was making a thin fog rise
from the ground, and the moon made it look like gray ghosts
floating through the air. The place was enchanting, with the
moon shining through the moss of the tall cypress trees and

painting a silver streak down the bayou and the river, with the gray mist twirling in the air. Skeeter felt that he was in another world from that of the day. He felt like standing up and floating through the air and becoming a part of the beautiful miracle he was seeing. It was a simple miracle, one that he had seen many times before and never noticed, the miracle of day changed into night, creating an entirely different world. He felt that he could look at the scene forever.

The reality of the trotline broke the spell for him, and he almost resented the line being in the river. He thought it was not right that something man had made should be in the midst of what he was seeing, something much greater and more beautiful than man could make. His resentment was soon erased as he felt a pulling when he touched the line. He had a fish, and now his mind was occupied with only the thought of getting the fish off the line. He was brought back from the night down to man's world again.

He pulled the skiff down the line until he reached the hook that held the fish. He raised it to the top of the water and pulled it into the boat. He went on down the line and removed two more fish. Then he went back to the house and put them into the box. He stood for a long time in the yard, looking towards the bayou, and wishing he could recapture the feeling that had picked him up, when he first went out into the night. But now it was gone, and he went into the house and went to bed.

The remainder of the days before Saturday were spent in the same way as the ones before had been—running the line early in the morning, watering the garden, bringing wood and water to the house, and drifting on the bayou and in the swamp. Finally Saturday came, and it was time to make the trip to town. Skeeter strung the fish the night before and was ready to leave at daybreak the next morning. Ma had his breakfast on the table when he got up and his lunch already fixed and in one of the croaker sacks.

"You be shore and git a pail of lard today," she said. "They ain't no more in the crock, and I done strained this we air usin' till hits plumb wore out. Hit jest won't last till hog killin' time."

"Air they anything else besides the meal, sugar, and coffee?" he asked. He hoped he could remember everything, for this was the first time he had ever had to remember what to get. Pa had always done that.

"You better git some salt, too," she said. "I shore hope yore Pa has 'nough money to git everthing. If'n they ain't enough, leave off the sugar."

He put the fish in the skiff and paddled down the bayou. The sun was turning the treetops red when he turned down the river. This was his first trip to town by himself, and it made him feel big and powerful. He knew that Pa would be proud that he had caught some fish, and he hoped they would bring enough money to buy the new netting.

He noticed a lot of things, as he drifted down the river alone, that he had never noticed before. He saw how the willows dipped into the water as if drinking, and how the leaves fell from the magnolia trees and were caught up by little whirlpools and spun round and round, like small boats, and then went skimming along with the current. He saw the gray squirrels bundle themselves into the moss of the cypress trees when they heard him make a sound, and become invisible to him. A mother coon brought her young to the edge of the river to drink the water, and then led them silently back into the woods. Ducks picked up and flew ahead of him, and the birds sat in the trees and chattered at him as he passed. Only the turtles sunning themselves on logs seemed unaware of his presence. They were conscious of nothing but the sun and the water. He paddled close to logs just to disturb their sleep and laughed when they rolled over into the water. It was like watching a parade of all the creatures of the river.

When he reached the docks, he tied the skiff and took the fish to the market. He had a hundred and fifty pounds, and was paid fifteen dollars. It was enough to buy the new netting, and it made him feel good thinking about it. He thanked Mr. Blanch and started down the lane to Uncle Jobe's shack. When he reached there, Uncle Jobe was sitting on the front porch.

"Good mornin', Massah Skeeter," he said. "Yore Pa won't be in from the mill till noon, so come in and sot a spell."

Skeeter greeted him and sat down on the porch. He felt in his pocket to be sure that the money was still there, for he didn't want to lose it before Pa came.

"I didn't bring you nothin' this time," said Skeeter.

"Thet's all right, child, I's powerful glad to see you without you bringin' me nothin'. I'm right pleased you sent yore pa to stay with me. I's fixed him up a good place to sleep, and we gits along jest fine. Hit does a old soul like me good to have company around, and yore Pa air sho' a fine man."

They sat and talked until noon, and shortly afterwards Pa came to the shack. He was glad to see Skeeter and slapped him on the back. Skeeter took out the lunch Ma had fixed for him, divided it three ways, and they ate dinner. Skeeter told him all about the fish he had sold, the traps being torn up, what his Ma had said to bring home, and everything that had happened during the past week. After they finished eating, Pa and Skeeter walked back to town.

"We better git them supplies and let you start back as soon as you kin," said Pa. "Hit'll take you a good whiles to git back by yoreself."

"I still got that fifty cents you give me one time when we had that good catch," said Skeeter, "and I wonder if'n I kin spend hit fer anything I wants now."

"Why shore you kin," said Pa. "Hits yore money and you kin do with hit as you please."

They went to the store and bought all the supplies Ma had wanted and the new netting for the traps. Skeeter bought himself a piece of lead pipe, three feet long and three inches wide. Pa didn't ask why he bought it, though he wondered what it was for. It was Skeeter's money, and if he wanted to spend it on lead pipe, that was his business. They took the supplies down to the docks and loaded them into the skiff. Pa told Skeeter good-by, and he started up the river. He didn't have as much time going back to watch things as he had coming down, for it was hard work for him to paddle the skiff up the river by himself. When he reached home, he was tired and his arms hurt, but he was proud that he had remembered and brought home everything Ma had told him.

TWELVE

SKEETER AND THERESA spent most of their time the next few days putting the new netting on the traps. It was slow work weaving the nets around the framing without leaving any holes or weak spots, and it took them many long hours before the work was done. When they finished, Skeeter decided not to put the traps back out, because the few fish he would catch would not be worth the chance of having the traps destroyed again. The cost was too high to repair them. He fished for bream along the edges of the swamp and used them for bait on the line and ran the line every night. This way he managed to keep a few fish in the fish box and have a little to take to town and sell.

He fastened the pipe he had bought into the bow of the skiff to use as a means of having light at night. He would cut the end of the pine torches down until they would fit into the pipe, and this way he would not need anyone to pole the skiff for him. Now he could go into the swamp by himself at night. He decided to bait the line with squirrel meat so that he wouldn't have to run it at night.

Skeeter had stopped taking his rifle when he went squirrel or rabbit hunting and would use only the knife. It was
very seldom that he missed a running rabbit or squirrel, and
he had practiced so much that he was accurate at over a
hundred feet. One day he hit a bird in midair, but he didn't
try throws like that very often. He seldom killed anything for
which he did not have a use.

One morning when he came in from running the line, Ma
told him that the wood supply was out and there was no
more pine under the house. He took the ax and went down
the river to cut some pine in the big woods. He hid the skiff
under some willow limbs and started through the thick buck
vines. This was the first time he had been in the woods by
himself, and he had a feeling of high adventure. He wanted
to bring his rifle with him, but he knew that it would only be
in the way bringing the wood back to the skiff. He would
have to make several trips into the woods before he had
enough.

He made his way through the thick growth and into the
part of the woods where the big pines were. He cut a chip
out of every tree on the way to be sure he would not lose
his way coming back and miss the place where he left the
skiff. He knew that he could find his way back to the river,
but he didn't want to do any extra walking carrying the load
of wood. He chopped the fat pine on the ground into sticks
and made several loads back to the skiff. Coming back with
his last load, he was working his way through some thick
vines when he heard strange noises in a clearing ahead of
him. When he remembered what Pa had said about the critters being mean during low water, he felt a little afraid. He
sat for a few minutes in silence thinking they would go
away, but the sounds became louder. He felt he had to see
what it was.

He lay flat on the ground and crawled on his stomach
through the vines, not daring to make a sound. It was slow

progress, and it was several minutes before he reached a place where he could see into the clearing. He lay in silence and watched the strange spectacle taking place before him. Two big bucks were on each side of the clearing facing each other. They turned and walked in opposite directions around the clearing, then stopped and faced each other again. They lowered their heads and charged straight at each other. Their antlers hit with a clash and knocked them both from their feet. They scrambled up and walked back to each side of the clearing, walking around again in opposite directions, looking like two boxers feeling each other out in the first round of a championship fight. When they walked half the circle around the clearing, they stopped, faced the center, charged in, and clashed antlers again, only this time they reared up and kicked with their front feet instead of falling to the ground. The third time they made the charge their antlers became entangled, and they fought around and around until they came loose. Then they went back to the edge of the clearing. The fourth time they made the charge they did not go back to the edge of the clearing but stayed in the middle of the circle and kicked and bit and slashed out at each other with their antlers. Skeeter knew that he was witnessing a death battle between two great bucks of the forest.

The bucks fought and struggled and rolled over and over on the ground and tore great gashes in each other's sides. Blood dripped to the ground, and they were both rapidly becoming spotted with blood. Skeeter's heart pounded wildly inside him, and his hands shook with fright. He wished that he had his rifle or that Pa was with him or that he was in the skiff in the bayou. He had never witnessed such a fight, not even the night in the woods when the Hooker boys had the bear wrestle. He wondered what they would do if they were here. He could not stand to watch the big, beautiful bucks slaughter each other, and yet he could not make himself leave. The fight was getting more vicious as it went along, and finally one of the bucks knocked the other to the ground and backed off to charge it with his antlers, to end its life, and the fight. Skeeter could stand it no longer, and he didn't know what he was doing he was so excited. He jumped to his feet and shouted wildly. He jumped up and down and shouted as loud as he could. The buck stopped his charge, and the one on the ground jumped to its feet. They both looked at Skeeter with surprise and bounded off through the vines in opposite directions.

Skeeter sat on the ground and wiped the sweat from his face with his hands. His face was red, and his heart was still pounding so hard that it hurt him. He couldn't understand what had made him do what he had done, because if one of the bucks had charged him it would have meant the end of his life. He had never been scared by Steel Head as he was by this fight, yet he knew that Steel Head was a much greater danger to him. It was just that he could not bear to see the beautiful, proud bucks end their lives in such a way. He would not mind hunting them and killing them for food, but he didn't want them to kill each other. He sat for a long time and rested and then returned to the skiff with the load of wood. He paddled slowly up the river to home.

When he had unloaded the wood and put it under the house, he carried some into the kitchen. His face was white as a sheet, and his hands shook.

"Whut in the world air wrong with you?" asked Ma. "You look like you seed a ghost over in them woods."

"Tain't nothin'," he said, and walked back into the yard.

He couldn't eat much dinner, and as soon as he finished he went to the woods next to the clearing to kill squirrels. When he returned, he dressed four for their supper and cut the others up for bait. He got into the skiff and went up the bayou and lay in the sun. He pulled off his clothes and swam in the water and then lay in the skiff and watched the clouds fly by overhead. He poled the skiff into the marsh grass so it could not drift and went to sleep.

He was awaked by the gentle patter of rain on his body. He did not know how long he had been asleep, but it was still light. Excitedly he poled the skiff down the bayou to the landing. Ma and Theresa were standing in the back yard in the rain; their clothes were soaked, but they were happy. The black clouds were rolling in from the south, and soon the whole sky would be covered. It was a weird sight, with the sun shining and rain falling at the same time. A giant rainbow was forming in the east. Skeeter got his meat and left to bait the hooks. The warm rain felt good to him, and he wished he could stay out in it all night. All memory of the fight he had witnessed that morning was gone now. When he got back to the landing, the sky was completely covered by the black clouds, and it was almost dark. Ma and Theresa were still standing in the rain. They went into the house and changed to dry clothes and started frying the squirrels for supper.

"Thank the Lord hit's come at last," said Ma. "That pore old parched ground would have blowed away afore long if'n hit hadn't got no water."

Skeeter was hungry now, and the supper tasted good to him. He ate until he could hold no more and then lay on his bed and listened to the rain beating against the roof. It had prevented his going into the swamp that night, but he didn't mind. The fish would bite good during the rainy night, and he liked to listen to the rain against the roof. Sleep came easy, and it was a sound sleep. When he awoke the next morning, the sun was out, and the black clouds were gone from the sky.

That was the last rain they had for many weeks. The days got hotter, and the ground was parched red. The fishing became so bad that Skeeter took the line from the river and stopped wasting the squirrels and the bream for bait. He kept meat on the table by killing game and catching the bream in the swamp, but if Pa had not been at the mill, they would have had nothing with which to cook them. Skeeter made many trips into the swamp at night, killing frogs, but he never got another chance at Steel Head. The big 'gator seemed to come out and do his killing and disappear into thin air.

The days changed into weeks, and finally the nights began to be cool, and the rains came more often. Early in the mornings there would be a chill in the air, and the swamp was filled with fog. The marsh grass turned brown, and the leaves on the trees became tinted with red. The days were shorter and the nights longer, and the river began to rise. There were not as many snakes about, and the baby squirrels were playing in the trees. The robins were starting their migration south, and bobwhite could be heard late in the afternoon calling the young into covey. The stalks of corn in the garden were turning yellow, and the blooms of the magnolia trees were dying and turning into seed. All the animals seemed to sense that fall was in the air, and the squirrels carried nuts and acorns into their dens all day. The big bullfrogs could be heard less often in the swamp at night, and the opossums were eating the last of the wild persimmon. The big bass were beginning to strike in the river, and the minnows stayed close to the bank. One night they heard the honking of wild geese flying overhead and knew that the warm days would soon be gone. Pa returned from the mill.

Pa and Skeeter set the traps and the line up the river, and the fishing was better. The gar and turtle were not as bad, and they managed to catch enough fish to buy all the supplies the family needed. By the first of November the river was back to normal, and the leaves were falling from the trees. Every day they could see hundreds of ducks flying into the edges of the swamp and the bayou and along the river. It would not be long until the deer meat was at its best, and the young quail were large enough for Skeeter to trap. The entire river and swamp looked like a new world every time the seasons changed.

A week before Thanksgiving the family was sitting at the table eating a supper of baked ducks that Skeeter had killed on the bayou.

"Let's bait up some turkeys and have the Hookers down fer a big dinner Thanksgivin'," said Pa. "They ain't never et down here, and we been up there so many times. I knows a good spot fer me and Skeeter to bait 'em up."

"I think that'd be a mouty fine thing to do," said Ma, "bein' as we took ever Sunday dinner up theer whiles you was at the mill, and they give us a lot uv eatin', too."

"Well, you start thinkin' 'bout the fixin's, Ma," he said, "and leave the turkey and the meats up to me and Skeeter. We'll start on that in the mornin'."

The next day when they left to run the traps, Pa carried an ear of corn and the hoe with them. Skeeter had never been on a baiting before, and he didn't understand it. When they got down the river, they tied the boat up and went into the big woods. Pa dug a shallow trench in the ground about six feet long and four inches wide, sprinkled kernels of the corn the length of the trench, and then they built a blind of pine boughs in the vines away from the trench. That afternoon they went back and the corn had not been touched, but when they went by the next morning it was gone, and there were turkey droppings on the ground. They baited the trench with corn for the next three days, and each morning when they went back the corn was gone. Then they stopped putting out the corn.

Pa and Skeeter rowed up the river and asked the Hookers about coming for the meal. The old man said they would be glad to and would bring plenty of whiskey. He wanted to know if there was anything else they needed, but Pa assured him that they had all the provisions.

Two days before the big day Pa and Skeeter went into the big woods and killed a young buck and brought him home. They dressed him and hung him in the kitchen to be barbecued. Ma had made several quarts of crab-apple jelly that week and had all her things ready to start cooking the dinner the next day. Early the next morning Pa and Skeeter went back to the trench in the woods and put corn in it again and hid behind the blind and waited.

"Now be shore and don't make no noise when they come," said Pa, "and don't miss no shot. You make the first throw with that knife, 'cause hit won't make no noise. Then when it hits one, if'n it does, be ready to shoot on the fly when the rest of them takes off."

They sat behind the blind for about an hour and nothing happened. Then they heard the slapping of big wings coming down through the trees, and nine turkeys lit on the ground and started eating the corn. Pa motioned for Skeeter to go ahead and throw, but Skeeter was a little slow in doing so. He had never wanted so much for his throw to count, for he wanted to show Pa that he could do it. He raised his arm and sent the knife straight into the breast of a turkey. When it hit, the turkey screamed, and the others took to the air. He threw up his rifle and shot almost at the same time as did Pa. They stepped from behind the blind and found three turkeys dead on the ground.

"Didn't think you could do hit," said Pa. "You must have learned a lot whiles I was gone last summer."

Skeeter didn't say anything, but he felt proud inside. They took the turkeys back to the house and dressed them and hung them beside the deer. Skeeter went out late that afternoon and killed a dozen ducks with the rifle and brought them home. Ma said if they didn't stop, the kitchen would be

so full they couldn't get inside and it would take her a year
to cook it all.

The family was up before dawn the next morning, preparing for the dinner. Ma had only one broiler big enough to
hold a turkey, so she would have to bake them one at a
time, and then there were all the ducks to bake. Pa and
Skeeter did not run the traps that morning, for they were
digging the pit in the back yard to barbecue the deer. When
the pit reached the depth of three feet, they cut small sweet
gum trees to lay over the top. Then they built a fire in the
pit with hickory limbs and put the deer on the sweet gum
poles. It would have to be watched all day to keep the fire
just right and keep the meat turned.

Ma baked the turkeys and the ducks in their own fat, and
then used the broth to make the dressing. She used corn
pone for the base of the dressing and mixed in sage and onions. She mixed three big pots of dressing and set them
aside to be cooked the next morning, so it would be hot for
the meal. It was late in the night when they stopped and
went to bed.

They were up again at dawn the next morning to finish
the preparations before the Hookers came. There was the
dressing to cook, the corn pone to make, and Ma was going
to make some big, sweet-potato pies. They did not have
enough plates for so many people, so Pa sent Skeeter up the
bayou to get giant lily pads to use instead. They wouldn't
need plates for anything but the dressing and the pie, so the
pads would do fine. It was a clear, warm day, so they moved
the table into the back yard to have the meal in the open.

It was midmorning when the Hookers arrived, and the
men had several jugs of whiskey and their guitars and fiddles
with them. They stayed in the yard and passed the jugs, and
the women went into the kitchen to finish the cooking. The
men talked and drank until the meal was ready and then

helped put all the food on the table. The deer was left on the pit so that everyone could go around and cut his choice piece, and they put the turkeys, the baked ducks, the dressing, corn pone, crab-apple jelly, and potato pies on the table. After Pa returned thanks, the meal was begun, and it lasted for over three hours. Then the boys went to sleep, and the old people went to the front porch to sit and talk. Sparky and Theresa walked into the woods to be alone.

"That's about the biggest feast that's ever been put on along Pearl River," said the old man. "I'm afeered that my britches air goin' to bust."

"It were about the best I ever seed," said the old woman.

"Well, I'm shore glad that you all enjoyed hit," said Pa. "We been owin' you a feed like this. I shore appreciate yore keepin' company with my family while I was gone this summer. Hit makes a body feel better to know his family air aroun' friends."

"Well, don't forget we're goin' to come by and take you all to the Christmas frolic in Mill Town with us," said the old man. "We been countin' on hit fer a long time."

"We'll be much obliged to go," said Pa.

They talked for a while and then all dozed off to sleep. They woke up late in the afternoon and the men went to the back yard. The two women stayed on the porch to talk. The jug was passed several more times, and then it was time to eat again. No one ate as much the second time as they had the first. When the second meal was finished, the boys started some music, and a dance was begun. They took turns dancing with the three women, and the jugs were passed so everyone was feeling good and happy. It was late at night when the Hookers bade their farewell.

THIRTEEN

THE DAYS were getting colder, and some mornings Pa and Skeeter had to wear their wool jackets while on the river. It was time for Skeeter to set his animal traps and almost time to kill the hogs. They were already making preparations for the hog killing. Pa and Skeeter were building a temporary smokehouse out of sweet gum poles and pine boughs and were getting a good supply of hickory logs together. They would kill the hogs the first morning there was a frost on the ground.

"I wish the frost would hurry and come," said Ma. "I got a hankerin' fer a bait of chitlins and cracklin' bread."

"Hit do sound good," said Pa. "The way the air felt this mornin' I believe the ground will be white in three or four days."

Skeeter went to the swamp that day and picked the places to set his traps. He had six of them, and he placed them on mudbanks and small islands of high ground around the edges of the swamp. If they didn't do good, he would move them around during the winter and try new places. He came back to the house and helped Pa sharpen the knives for the hog killing.

The nights were cold now, and the quilts felt good to Skeeter. He liked to sleep rolled up in a ball like a squirrel, and he hated to get out of bed in the morning. Late that night he heard a noise come from the hog pen, and the hogs squealed loudly. He jumped from the warm bed and slipped on his clothes. Pa had heard it too, and he dressed and came into the room with his gun. They lit a torch on the hearth and slipped into the yard and down to the pen. They found one of the hogs dead and badly torn and heard a splashing up the bayou.

"Hit's that kill-crazy 'gator agin," said Pa. "I wished I could git a bead on that varment with this gun. I'd blow them loco brains of his'n all over them marsh flats."

"Let's go git him now," said Skeeter. "He couldn't be too fer off time we gits started."

"Tain't no use runnin' that varment in the dark," said Pa. "He knows the swamp a heap better'n we do."

They climbed into the pen and examined the dead hog. The big 'gator had mangled it badly.

"They's still some good left," said Pa. "We kin cook out the lard and git the chitlins, and maybe a little meat. You run to the house and git the knives and we'll gut him now so'es he won't spoil till mornin'."

Skeeter ran to the kitchen to get the knives, while Pa brought the hog to the back stoop. Ma and Theresa were in the kitchen.

"Whut were hit?" asked Ma.

"Old Steel Head done got another one of the hogs," said Skeeter. "But Pa says they's still some good left on him. We's goin' to gut him now."

"I knowed that varment would come back," said Ma. "Hit ain't safe fer a body to be outside at night with that devil around."

"Tain't that bad," said Skeeter. "That's the fust time he's been around here in a long time."

"But hit shore won't be the last," said Ma. "He'll git us all afore he's done with it."

"I'm goin' to see if'n I kin git him tomorrow," said Skeeter.

He took the knives to the stoop, and they hung the hog up and dressed it as best as they could. It was hard to clean being torn up so badly. When they finished, they washed the blood from their hands and went back to bed.

Skeeter and Pa were up earlier than usual the next morning to run the traps and line, and when they returned home, Ma and Theresa had already started on the hog. They scalded it with hot water, scraped it, and then removed the skin and fat to fry down as lard. The rest of the meat they would grind up as sausage. Skeeter got his knife and his rifle, filled one of his pockets with shells, found half of a corn pone in the kitchen and put it in his pocket, and went down to the landing and got into the skiff.

"You be kerful in that swamp," shouted Pa, "and be shore and git out of there afore hit gits dark." Pa was not afraid for Skeeter, because he knew that he could take care of himself during the day.

Skeeter poked the skiff up the bayou and tried to think of every place that the 'gator might be in the daytime. He figured that it would be asleep and he could slip up on it. He made long sweeps along the edges and then worked his way further into the swamp. He raked his pole along logs and in grassy spots and looked around all the mudbanks and cypress knees.

The swamp had taken on a desolate look with the coming of winter. The trees no longer had leaves, and the vines were bare. Only the moss on the cypress broke the monotony of limbs against sky. The sky was cloudy that day, and the grayness gave an eerie atmosphere to the already dismal surroundings.

Skeeter worked his way back and forth along the swamp with no sign of the 'gator, and when he thought it was noon, he stopped and ate his corn pone. He drank some of the swamp water, and it didn't taste good, so he swallowed a little and spit the rest out. A fine mist was beginning to fall, so he pulled the collar of his jacket tight around his neck and continued his relentless search for the alligator.

He pushed deeper and deeper into the swamp, and he was already farther in than he had ever been before. The trees were much thicker and the vines more entangling, and the water was getting shallow. Sometimes he had to lie in the bottom of the skiff to pass under the vines, and he could hear an occasional snake, that was late in hiding away for the approaching cold winter, dropping into the water ahead of him. Even the water was changing color. It was turning from black to green, and the green slime covered the top so that he could not see past the surface. An irresistible force pushed him farther and farther into the swamp. Many times he found himself trapped by vines, and he would have to back the skiff out and go another way. The sickening stench of the slime was so bad that he could hardly bear it, but he pushed on and on. The vines and the trees and dead limbs were so thick that he could not see the sky, and he did not know what time it was. The mist was beginning to soak down through the trees, and he was wet and cold, so he decided to give up the hunt for the day. He started back and then realized that he was lost, and the sun was gone from the sky. The thick trees and the clouds had fooled him, and he had not realized that it was so late. In a few minutes the last gleam of light would be gone and there would be no moon or stars to guide him out. He didn't know what to do. He was scared, and he was wet and hungry, and his mouth ached for a drink, but he dared not drink the slimy water.

He realized for the first time that this was what men feared most—being lost in the swamp at night.

The mist was turning into rain, and he poled the skiff under some thick vines to escape as much of the rain as possible. When the last light was gone, he became engulfed in a great sea of darkness, a darkness that would even bring terror to a man's heart. He wished he were in his warm bed or that he would wake up and find that this was only a bad dream. He wished that he could jump up and fly from the swamp, but he knew that his condition was hopeless, and no amount of wishing could get him out. He lay down and tried to sleep, but sleep would not come. He saw a pair of green eyes coming at him through the trees, and when they were above him they stopped, and something screamed. It was a panther, and the scream made the flesh crawl on his bones. He picked up his rifle and aimed what he thought was the sight, at the eyes. He would shoot if it came at him, but it did not. It continued its journey through the night and was soon gone. Skeeter lay on his back and soon fell asleep from sheer exhaustion.

His eyes had been closed only a few minutes when he felt something drop across his neck. It was round and cold, and he knew that it was a snake, but he dared not move for fear it would strike. He could feel its smooth body slowly inching across his face. Cold sweat broke from his face, and his blood turned to ice. The snake was making a coil on his neck because it liked the feel of his warm body. Skeeter knew what was happening, and he wanted to jump up and scream, but he also knew that one strike from the snake would mean sure death. His hands shook, and he tried to stop them for fear it would shake the skiff. He looked into the blackness above him, trying not to think. Sweat was pouring from his face, and he thought he would go crazy at any moment. Finally, he felt the snake's body move again, and it moved slowly across his neck. He heard a splash in the water, and it was gone.

Now sleep was out of the question. He sat in the skiff and shook, and his heart pounded madly, until at last the streaks of light broke through the haze, and it was dawn. He had never seen a dawn that was so beautiful to him. His stomach ached from hunger, and his throat was dry, but it was light, and he was not afraid any more. He could not stand the thirst any longer, so he raked the green slime from the surface and drank some of the water. The stench would not stay on his stomach, and he retched it back up. It made him feel sick, and his head hurt. He eyes were red from lack of sleep and his clothes were soaked with water. He looked at the moss on the trees to tell directions, and then started his slow journey back through the swamp. He did not think of Steel Head on the way back; his only thought was of getting out. He had to turn around many times and backtrack, and it was almost dark when he reached familiar ground and knew that he was out. He poled the skiff to the bayou and down to the landing. He was weak and sick, but he knew that he had been where no man had ever been before, and possibly would never be again. He picked up his gun and went into the house. Pa grabbed him, and Ma and Theresa were crying.

"You done give us the biggest skeer we ever had," said Pa. "If'n I weren't so glad to see you I'd whale the daylights out'n you. Where you been all this time in that swamp?"

"Lookin' fer Steel Head, but I didn't git him," was all that he said.

He took a big drink of the clean fresh water in the bucket and then put on dry clothes. Ma fixed him a bowl of hot gruel and a corn pone, and he ate it slowly to keep from retching it up. The warm food settled his stomach, and he felt better. He got in the bed and rolled up in the warm covers, and the bed never felt so good to him before in his life. He immediately fell into a deep sleep.

"I shore thought we had lost our last son," said Pa. "Hit would be mouty hard without him."

"He's got to quit doin' things like that," said Ma.

FOURTEEN

A FEW DAYS LATER, the frost was on the ground, and it was time to kill the last hog. Ma and Theresa heated the water, while Pa and Skeeter killed it. They scalded and scraped it and hung it up to bleed; and before the day was through they had cut up the fat and skin for lard, separated the hams, shoulders, backbone, ribs, and all the scraps they would use for sausage. The next day they would pack the meat in salt to prepare it for smoking with hickory limbs. Then they would use part of the intestines for sausage casings and save the rest to fry as chitterlings. When the sausage was ground and stuffed, they would hang the casings beside the hams to be smoked, cook backbone and ribs and store them in the fat, and make cheese from the head. It would be soaked in vinegar and called souse. That night Ma mixed up the crisp pieces of skin with the corn pone and cooked the chitterlings, and they ate till there was none left. They would save most of the meat for the flood season when they could not get outside.

Pa and Skeeter ran the traps and line every morning, and when they returned, Skeeter would run his animal traps. When he caught a mink, he would tack its pelt to the house to dry. The days passed on, and soon it was Christmas time. Pa cut a small cedar tree and put it in the house, and they decorated it with bits of bright paper and cloth left over from the dresses. There was no money for presents, but Ma had planned to have a good dinner, and the trip to Mill Town would be enough. The two red dresses were finished and hanging on the wall to be worn to the frolic. The Christmas frolic was the only time during the year that the townspeople would let the swamp rats join in their festivities, and they looked forward to it through the year. It was held in the one-room school, where there was dancing and food, and the men would have jugs of whiskey to pass around. Theresa could hardly wait until Christmas Eve.

Each family was supposed to bring food, so Pa and Skeeter baited the turkey trench again, and the day before Christmas Eve they killed two turkeys. Ma baked one to take to the frolic and saved one for their Christmas dinner. There was not much sleep that night, for everyone was too excited.

They were up at dawn the next morning, hurrying to get the housework done, the traps run, and the final preparations for the trip made. After dinner, Ma and Theresa put on their new dresses, and Pa put on his best pants and shirt. They made Skeeter put on a clean pair of overalls. Theresa combed her long hair and tied a white ribbon in the back— she was beautiful. She hoped Sparky would be proud of her. About midafternoon the Hookers came, and they all loaded into the boats and started the trip down. Pa thought he had never seen as many jugs of whiskey as there were in the boats. There was hardly enough room for the passengers. The men emptied one jug on the way down.

When they arrived at the docks, there were many boats tied to the pilings, and there were a lot of people on the streets. Wagons were rolling into town, and there were many horses and mules tied to the hitching posts. The people from all the surrounding territory were coming in for the frolic. Everyone seemed in a joyous mood, and much talk and laughter were heard on the street. The women took the food and went on to the schoolhouse, while the men stayed on the street to talk with friends they had not seen for a long time. The Hooker men passed the jugs to a number of people on the street, and a good deal of conversation went around. When it started getting dark, all the men went to the schoolhouse.

The food was laid out on long tables on the school grounds, and there were oil lamps around for light. There was every kind of food a person could imagine: turkeys, venison, chickens, fish, ducks, big pots of dressing, potato salad and baked sweet potatoes, many different kinds of pies and cake, and big tubs of coffee for the women and children. Tin plates and forks were stacked high; everyone could pass by and get what food he wanted, then get off in little groups of his own. The eating went on for several hours, then the preachers said a few words of welcome and about Christmas, and all the folks went inside for the frolic. Most of the young boys stayed on the outside to play and fight and tear the good clothes that their mothers had fixed for them.

The inside of the school was decorated with holly and pine, and mistletoe hung over the door. Some of the boys would stand by the door and try to kiss the young girls as they came inside. The girls would giggle and try to stop them.

Chairs were placed around the outside of the large room so the old folks could sit and watch, and for the people who didn't want to dance. Lanterns were swung from the roof, and the old, pot-bellied, iron stove in the corner was red with the glowing coals of a warm fire.

One end of the room contained a platform for the string band, and the fiddlers were already taking their places. There were several fiddles and guitars, and one bass fiddle. The fiddlers were tuning up their instruments, and the drone of the waiting crowd drowned out all sound. People were laughing and talking, and the dancers were lining up their partners for the first dance. Theresa had many offers for the first dance, but she would have no one but Sparky.

The caller climbed to the platform and raised his arms for silence. Everyone faced the front and listened.

"Now git yore pardner, and let's git ready for the lead out," he shouted.

Everyone got his partner, and they lined up facing each other. Those who were not going to be in the dance backed off the floor and took the chairs around the room. Each member of the band stood up, and after they played the first few notes of a tune, they stopped. The caller sang out:

> Git yore pardner,
> Swing her around,
> Come on now
> And go to town.
> Right foot up,
> Left foot down,
> Come on now
> And swing her around.

Then the dance was started. The two lines of men and women came to the center and bowed and skipped back. They came back and locked arms and swung to the left, then skipped back, then returned and swung to the right, and then did do se do and started swinging down the line. When the dance was finished, new sets took the floor. The men went outside to drink from the jugs, and the spirit of the frolic grew as each new set of dancers took the floor.

As Skeeter entered, the three Smith brothers stopped him.

"Ain't you a Corey?" one of them asked.

"Yeah!" said Skeeter.

"I thought you was a brother to the bastard whut run off with our sister," he said. "Let's rough him up a little, boys."

One of them shook Skeeter, and another slapped him. Sparky and Theresa were dancing on that end of the floor, so they saw what was happening. They dropped out of the dance, and Sparky went over and said something to the rest of the Hooker boys. They all crossed the room toward the door.

The three men were still shaking and slapping Skeeter, so without saying a word, the Hooker boys made a circle around them. Sun Up and Sun Down grabbed one of the boys and threw him through the glass window before he knew what had happened. Glass and window framing shattered all over the end of the room. The music stopped and a few women screamed. Then the caller jumped to the platform, the music started again, and the dance went on. A fight was nothing new at the frolic.

The Hooker boys dragged the other two brothers out the door and picked the third up from the ground. Pa and Old Man Hooker and a lot of other men followed them outside. A crowd had already formed around them. Sun Up explained to Pa and the old man what had happened.

"Well, them yellow varments," said the old man, "pickin' on a little feller like Skeeter." He turned and faced the crowd. "If'n they's ary of these fellers' friends here that wants to git in this, you mout as well step up now."

All of the Smith brothers' friends looked at the Hooker boys, and nobody moved.

"Well, git their pants down, boys," said the old man.

The Hooker boys held the brothers and dropped their pants to the ground. They bent them over, and the old man came around with his belt. He took them one at a time and strapped them twenty licks each. They let the brothers pull their pants back up, but they kept the circle around them. Laughter could be heard in the crowd.

"I 'spect their ends air a little hot," said the old man. "We better carry 'em down to the river and cool 'em off a bit."

They dragged the brothers—by their feet—down to the boat docks. The crowd and Pa and Skeeter followed. When they got to the end of the dock, all the Hookers stopped and passed the jug.

"We'll git even with you damned swamp rats," said one of the brothers.

"We ain't worried 'bout the likes of you none," said the old man. "But jest fer sayin' that, I think the boys had better have a little contest. The oldest of you boys divide into teams of fours and see who kin throw one each of these yellow bastards the furtherest in the river, and then the team that wins kin throw the last one in. And afore the contest starts, I want to say a word." He turned to the three brothers. "If'n we ever hear of you sons of bitches botherin' a Corey agin, they'll be iron weights tied to yore backs next time we throws you in the river. Now start the contest."

Four of the boys took the first brother by the hands and feet, swang him back and forth a few times, and sent him tumbling, end over end, into the cold, muddy water. They could hear him come up snorting and fighting for the bank. This was repeated until all three had been deposited in the river. Then all the people went back and joined the dance.

It was well after the hour of midnight when the dancing stopped and the people started their journeys home. Ma and Theresa were very happy because they had made nearly every one of the dances. They were tired, and yet the trip was beautiful. The moon was high above the trees, and it made the muddy water of the river change to silver and gold. Sparky and Theresa sat in the back of one of the boats and made a wish on the Christmas moon, which was supposed to come true.

*   *   *

The Coreys got up late the next morning, ate a light breakfast, and Ma put the turkey and dressing on the hearth to bake for their big meal that night. Skeeter ran his animal traps, but they let the fish traps and the line go since this was to be a day of rest and pleasure.

In the middle of the afternoon they were sitting on the front porch when they saw a boat turn up the bayou from the river. A man was rowing, and a woman was sitting in the back. When it got closer, they saw that it was Jeff and Clarise. Pa and Skeeter jumped to their feet and ran into the house.

"Hit's Jeff and Clarise comin' up the bayou in a boat!" cried Pa.

Ma and Theresa stopped their cooking, and they all ran to the landing to wait for the boat. When it touched the bank, Jeff and Clarise jumped out, and there was much hugging and kissing and warm greetings. They went into the house and sat in the kitchen.

"We jest come to spend Christmas Day," said Jeff. "We got to catch the boat back in the mornin'."

"Tell us all about yoreself," said Pa. "We ain't heerd a word from you since the two of you been gone."

"We're livin' up at Monticello," said Jeff, "and I'm workin' in the mill. The pay's a heap better then hit air down at Mill Town. Clarise air workin' in a store, and we live in one of the mill houses. We likes hit jest fine."

"We's mouty glad to hear that, son," said Pa.

"We had to slip off the boat down at Mill Town and borrow this boat so'es we wouldn't have no trouble with them brothers of Clarise's," said Jeff.

"You don't need never to worry about that again," said Pa. "Last night down at the frolic they tried to ruff up Skeeter, and them Hooker boys got 'um and pulled their pants down and whopped their butts with a belt, and then they throwed 'em in the river. Old Man Hooker told 'em that if'n they ever messed with any of us again, they would throw 'em in the river with iron weights on their backs."

"Serves them right," said Clarise.

"I shore wish you could have been there, Jeff," said Pa.

Ma and Theresa finished the cooking, and then they had the big supper. When it was finished, they sat around and talked and sang Christmas songs until late in the night. Pa moved in and slept with Skeeter, and Ma moved in with Theresa, so Jeff and Clarise could have the big room to themselves. Pa said that this was the best Christmas he had ever spent, and they all agreed.

FIFTEEN

THE DAYS OF THE SUN were now gone, and as the weeks wore on, the days were darker and drearier. There was fog on the river every morning, and the sky was filled with clouds. The wind blew from the north, and it was cold, so it made Pa and Skeeter shiver as they went about their daily work of running traps and lines. Sometimes there was ice along the edges of the river and bayou; there was frost on the ground nearly every morning. The piles of wood did not last as long, and they had to make more and more trips into the big woods. The singing birds were gone, and they did not often see the squirrels. The nights were long, and the days were short. The snakes had disappeared completely from the swamp, and many times the trees were covered with ice. The dead limbs would break from the weight of the ice, fall into the water, and it was always a danger to Skeeter when he went under the trees. Great swarms of blackbirds flew around the clearing and the woods, and ducks were plentiful on the bayou.

153

The trips to town were no longer a pleasure to Pa and Skeeter for it was cold, and the wind went through their clothes, chilling their bones until they ached. The vegetables had long been gone from the garden, and since the wild poke salat was also gone, there were no greens of any kind on the table to eat. But the deer were plentiful, and this was the best time of the year to kill them. The meat was sweet and thickly coated with fat. There were plenty of ducks, and they could still now and then kill the rabbits and the squirrels, and sometimes Skeeter killed the blackbirds and Ma made pies of them. They were good, stewed tender with plenty of dumplings. Winter was not too bad in the swamps, except for the wind and the cold.

Skeeter was running his animal traps in the morning and the afternoon for fear of losing a catch, because it would not be long before he had to take the traps up. The rains would come in March, and they would have to go to Fort Henry and sell the pelts before then. They depended on the money to buy supplies to last them during the flood. The Hookers did not come by as often, because many days the weather was too bad to be on the river, and they could not take their whiskey to Mill Town.

One afternoon Pa went with Skeeter to run the animal traps. It was bitterly cold, and the swamp was filled with mist and fog rising from the water. The sky was cloudy, and it looked as if it would sleet, so they hurried from one trap to another. The first traps had nothing, but in the last they had caught a mink. Skeeter removed the animal and reset the trap. This trap was the farthest one in the swamp, and it was a long way from home; so Skeeter poled the skiff as fast as he could through the vines and cypress knees. It looked as if the clouds were flying through the tops of the trees. Pa pulled his jacket tight and wished that he had stayed at home. Skeeter brought the skiff through a group of knees and made a sharp turn along the mudbank and had almost passed it when he dug the pole into the muck and stopped. Pa looked up and saw that Skeeter's hands were shaking, and Skeeter motioned for him to look at the mudbank. Pa saw the top of a giant 'gator head with a piece of steel sticking from it. Steel Head was asleep on the mudbank, and had not heard them coming. Skeeter picked up the rifle and aimed, but then he put it back down.

"Whut's the matter with you?" asked Pa. "Go ahead and shoot whiles you got the chance."

"I started hit with a piece of steel," said Skeeter, "and I'm goin' to finish hit that way. You take the rifle, and if'n I don't kill him, then shoot."

Skeeter took his long hunting knife from his belt. He drew back the blade and threw it with all the force of his body. He had never thrown the knife so hard before, and he almost fell from the skiff. The blade buried to the hilt in the 'gator's head, just below the frog gig. Steel Head flopped over twice on the mudbank and lay dead.

Skeeter didn't trust the big 'gator even in death. He took the rifle and shot it between the eyes, then reloaded and shot it again. He would have shot again, if Pa had not told him he was wasting shells and to stop. He sat in the skiff for a few minutes and didn't say anything. He thought of the dead hogs, of the many nights and days he had hunted the 'gator, of the night he spent in the swamp and nearly lost his own life, and now the end had come so easily. He had always thought of it as being a death struggle with the 'gator, but Steel Head had not known what had hit him. It was too easy, and he almost wished he had not seen the 'gator, so that he could have tracked it down and engaged it in combat. Pa seemed to understand what was going on in his mind, for he sat in the cold wind and mist and didn't say anything. Finally Skeeter poled the skiff back to the landing.

Taking a coil of rope, they went back to the swamp in the rowboat. They tied the rope around Steel Head and pulled him from the bank, then dragged him back to the landing. He was so heavy they had to pull him up the bank an inch at a time. Ma and Theresa came out and looked and went back into the house.

When they finally got him to the back yard, they measured him; he was twenty-two feet long. Then they rolled him on his back and split him open with an ax; Skeeter pulled out his knife and worked on him. They removed all the meat and bones and threw it in the bayou, then scraped until they had all the flesh from the hide. It was dark and had started sleeting, so they went into the house and left the 'gator until morning, when they could finish with him. Ma, Pa, and Theresa were in a mood of celebration, but for some reason Skeeter did not feel as they did. He had wanted to fight the 'gator as the big bucks had fought, to slash out at each other, to tear each other until the water was red with blood, and one of them had died and sunk into the muck of the swamp. But when he remembered that it was he who had caused Steel Head to go crazy, and everything that the 'gator had killed was his fault, he was glad that it was dead—even if the end had come in the way that it had. He went in and joined in the supper, and the worries left his mind.

The next morning when they finished cleaning the hide, Skeeter pulled the gig from the alligator's head. They cut out all the meat from the neck and head, leaving the head attached to the hide. Pa said it would be best to take it to Fort Henry for it would be worth more there, so they stored it under the house.

The work was the same day after day, and the weather stayed misty and cold. Skeeter longed for the hot summer days when he could drift in the skiff and swim naked in the bayou. He would be glad when the flood came, for he wouldn't have to go out of the house. He could sit by the hearth in the kitchen, eat, and then sleep and be warm.

One day when they were up the river, Pa took up the trotline, pulled the traps into the boat, and brought them home. He told Skeeter it was time to take up the animal traps, for they would have to make the trip to Fort Henry in plenty of time, before the flood came. When Skeeter made his rounds that day, he brought the traps home with him and put them back under his bed.

"Hit's goin' to be too hard fer you and me to make that long a trip up the river by ourselves," said Pa. "Let's go up to the Hookers tomorrow and see when they air goin' next, and maybe we kin go with them."

"I think that's the right thing to do," said Ma. "You and Skeeter could never row that boat all the way to Fort Henry by yoreself."

The next morning they rowed up the river to the Hookers and asked about the trip. The old man insisted that they stay for dinner.

"We's goin' to run up a load in three days," he said, "and we'll be more then glad to have you go with us."

"Will hit be all right if'n we tow our boat behind with our pelts and supplies?" asked Pa.

"Shore hit will," he said. "Them boys could tow a barge if'n they had a mind to. And you kin bring Glesa and Theresa up here, and they kin stay till we gits back. Hit wouldn't be good to leave them down to yore place with all this bad weather we is havin'. I'm leavin' Sparky and No Moon to look after things."

"Now that's a right good idea," said Pa, "and I shore do appreciate yore invite."

"Be shore to bring some kever to take on the trip," he said, "fer hit'll take us two nights sleepin' out on the trip up, with the river gittin' swift like hit air. Hit gits mighty cold on the river at night."

Pa and Skeeter stayed for dinner and then returned home. They spent all the next day bringing pine from the big woods, so the work would not be so hard when they returned, and the following day they made ready for the trip. They rolled the pelts into little bundles and put them in croaker sack. Ma made them a bundle of sausage, corn meal, and strips of dried fish. There would be no need to take any cooking utensils, for the Hookers would have plenty.

The next morning they rolled their quilts into bundles and were on their way up the river before daylight.

The 'gator hide was so large it couldn't be put in the boat, so they tied it in the skiff and pulled it behind. The river was swift, and the boat was overloaded; it was hard work for Pa and Skeeter to row against the current. There was ice along the river, and the cold wind burned their faces. Ma and Theresa shivered in their thin cotton dresses. But despite the cold, Pa and Skeeter were sweating when they reached the Hooker landing.

They went into the house, were greeted by the old man and woman, and sat by the fire to warm. The boys were preparing for the trip, so Pa and Skeeter went back to the landing and moved the 'gator hide into the boat so they would be ready to leave when the others had finished. The fire was warm and felt good to them, and they hated to leave when the Hooker boys came in and told them it was time to go.

Pa got into the boat with the old man, Skeeter got into the other one, and they tied Pa's boat behind and started up the river. Both boats were heavily loaded, but the Hooker boys didn't seem to mind. Their backs and arms were hard from the many trips they had made up the river, and they fought the current with steady determination.

"Where in tarnation did you git sech a 'gator hide?" asked the old man.

"That's the loco 'gator what's been givin' us sech a bad time," said Pa. "Killed two of the hogs afore we got him. Skeeter killed him the other day with his knife."

"You mean that youngin' killed that big 'gator with a knife?"

"He shore did," said Pa. "Buried hit up to the hilt in its head. That boy beats ary thing I ever seed throwin' that thing."

"Well, I'm shore glad he's yore boy and a friend," said the old man. "I'd ruther be shot betwix the eyes with a gun then stuck with a knife. I'm jest downright skeered of them things."

"I don't think Skeeter would ever hurt ary man," said Pa.

At noon they pulled the boats to the bank to eat a cold dinner that the old man had brought. They rested a few minutes and moved on. The day was getting colder, and Skeeter sat in the boat and shivered, thinking of warm fires and his comfortable bed at home. Their progress was very slow, for they were fighting directly into a strong north wind. Skeeter didn't see how the Hooker boys could keep such a steady pace, but their oars never faltered for a moment. They bent forward and backward, their oars touching the water, pulling, and then coming out, shoving the boat forward a little at a time. Occasionally they would stop and take a deep drink of whiskey to warm their bodies and their spirits as well.

When the light began to fade away, they stopped at the foot of a bluff to make camp for the night. The top of the bluff was covered with tall magnolia trees, so they made camp under them to keep off some of the mist. A big fire was built, and they cooked a supper of salt pork, grits, and corn pone. The men drank some of the whiskey, then piled enough logs on the fire to keep it burning all night. They laid out their bedding in a circle around the fire. The Hookers did not stay up all night and play as they did on the fox hunt, for they were tired, and soon everyone went to bed. Skeeter rolled up in his quilt on the cold ground, tried to get warm, then moved closer to the fire and was soon asleep.

They were up by daybreak the next morning cooking breakfast and breaking up the camp. Skeeter was stiff from sleeping on the ground, but the Hookers didn't seem to be bothered by it. They cooked the sausage Pa had brought and made a corn pone. They boiled coffee in a big bucket, and the smell mixed well with the cold morning air. When breakfast was done, they put out the fire and moved on again.

The banks of the river changed appearance as they moved further north. There was not much swamp along the banks; sometimes they passed fields and meadows running right down to the water. There were hills, then long flats, and then great stretches of the swamp again. The pines grew closer to the river; sometimes they passed fields and meadows running right down to the water; sometimes they saw cottonfields lying idle or cows grazing along the river. But they never went too far at a time without seeing stretches of swamp, and the water was just as muddy and brown as it was at Mill Town. There were many ducks on the river, and Skeeter shot them as they moved along that afternoon. When it was time for them to stop to make camp, he had twelve in the boat.

They picked a thick pine grove along the river to make their camp that night. They built the fire, then cut small pine saplings to make lean-tos to sleep in. They covered the lean-tos with pine boughs and piled pine straw inside them. The pine trees were green all year, and their branches made a good roof when in the woods at night. After this was finished, they cleaned the ducks and roasted them with sticks over the fire. When they finished eating, they went to bed. The lean-tos were warm and kept out the cold wind, so the sleep was much better that night.

By noon the next day they reached the outskirts of Fort Henry. At the south end of town there was the mill that most river towns had, the mill houses, and then the Negro shacks. The boat docks were a half mile up the river from the mill, and there were many more docks than there were at Mill Town. There were several big docks for the steamboats, and wharves along the bank on which to stack the cotton and other goods that were shipped out on the river. They tied their boats to a dock and started unloading.

"Let's go uptown and git us rooms at the hotel afore we sells ary a thing," said the old man. "I looks forward to this trip ever time so'es I kin sit on one of them water fountains and git under one of them spigots of hot water and soap myself."

"Hit suits me jest fine," said Pa, "but we better sell this 'gator hide fust, cause hit's too big to tote around."

"Well, we'll leave the boys here to watch the stuff, and me and you and Skeeter'll go and sell hit."

They took the hide and carried it up the street to one of the trading posts, and the boys stayed on the docks. The street was much wider and had many more stores than the one at Mill Town. There were all kinds of shops and many saloons and show houses. The street was crowded with wagons and horses, and many people were on the sidewalks. A lot of people stopped and looked at the big 'gator hide as they passed, for they had never seen one so large before. Pa, Skeeter, and the old man carried it through the door of one of the big trading posts, and the owner came over to them.

"You let me handle this, Abner," whispered the old man. "I knows how to handle these fellows."

"That shore is a big one," said the man. "Is it for sale?"

"Hit's fer sale if'n you wants hit bad enough," said the old man.

"I'll give you twenty-five dollars," he said.

"You must want to buy jest the tail," said the old man. "They ain't many 'gators like this whut allows theyselves to git kilt."

"Well, I'll make it thirty," said the man.

"Now, ain't that jest dandy," said the old man. "Let's take hit somewhere else, boys."

He reached down as if to pick up the hide, and the man stopped him.

"Forty," he said.

"Now that sounds better," said the old man. "Make hit fifty and you got yoreself a hide. Otherwise, we's jest wastin' our time."

"Well, all right, I'll make it fifty," said the man. "You swamp rats give me a pain in the head sometimes."

He pulled out his wallet and counted out five ten-dollar bills and handed them to the old man. They went out to the street, and he handed the money to Pa.

"You see," he said, "you jest got to know how to handle them fellers."

"Well, I shore am proud," said Pa, "and I thanks you a lot."

When they were gone, the owner motioned for two clerks to help him carry the hide to the back of the store.

"I would have given a hundred dollars for a hide like this," he said. "It'll bring two hundred in Jackson."

They walked back to the docks to gather up all their supplies and goods and then went back up the street to get a room at the hotel. When they went in, the old man went up to the counter.

"Give us four rooms with big beds," he said, "and make 'em close to the water fountains and hot-water spigots."

"You mean toilets and showers," said the clerk. "Just sign here, please, and pay in advance."

The old man marked an X on the book and paid for the rooms. Pa tried to pay for his and Skeeter's, but the old man wouldn't let him. The clerk handed him the keys, and a Negro went with them to show them where the rooms were. They went inside and put all their bedding and supplies on the floor. The old man came back down to Pa's room.

"We's goin' to sell our whiskey now," he said, "but we'll save out enough to tide us over till we gits back. We's got a regular customer here that buys all we brings, so we won't have to shop around. You and Skeeter go on and sell yore pelts and meet us back here in a hour. You kin take them pelts back to the place where we sold the 'gator hide, and don't let him gyp you."

The Hookers went out with their jugs of whiskey, and Pa and Skeeter took the sack of pelts back to the trading post. They had twenty-five mink and otter pelts, and the man offered Pa a hundred dollars. Pa thought that was a good price so he took it. He thanked the man and they went back to the hotel. They waited a few minutes, and the Hookers returned.

"Let's all take one of them hot soapings and then go out and et and do the town," said the old man. "I got a hankerin' fer a bellyful of good beef steak."

Pa agreed, and they all went into the shower room at one time. They turned on only the hot water, and then took off their clothes and got under it. There were several big bars of soap in a bucket, so they passed them around and soaped each other until the floor was covered with soap suds.

"This water air hot enough to scald a hog," said the old man, "but I shore do likes it."

"I like it too," said Pa. "This air the fust time I ever stood under one of these hot-water spigots."

When they finished, the room was so full of soap suds and steam that it was almost dangerous for a person to go inside. They dressed and went outside the hotel. It was dark, and the lamps were lighted in the shop windows and along the street. They walked down the sidewalk and into a restaurant and sat at a long table. A waiter came over to them.

"Give us all one of the biggest beef steaks you got in the house," said the old man, "and bring plenty of them fried tators. Sun Up, you go back to the hotel and git a jug of whiskey. I wants to wet my whistle afore I eats."

Sun Up left and was back presently with a jug of whiskey. They passed it around the table. The waiter came over and placed knives, forks, and spoons at each place.

"What'll you folks have to drink?" he asked.

"We brought our own whiskey," said the old man. "Thank ye jest the same."

The waiter stared at the old man and then returned to the kitchen. In a few minutes he returned with the steaks and a big plate of fried potatoes.

"Don't know why he brought these knives," said the old man. "I don't never use 'em eatin' steak. I always said that if'n you had to use a knife to cut a piece of steak, hit weren't fitten to eat."

He picked up the steak with his hands and started eating. All the rest did the same. They grabbed handfuls of the potatoes and crammed in their mouths and ate a slice of bread with one bite. When they finished, they smacked their lips and all took a big drink of whiskey.

"I know where they's a good stage show," said the old man. "Do everbody want to see it?"

"I'd like to," said Skeeter. "I ain't never seed one."

"I'd like hit too," said Pa.

All the boys said they would go, so they went up the street to one of the show houses. The seats were nearly filled, so they had to sit in the back. There was a long aisle between the rows of seats, and the stage was at the rear of the building. Lamps were along both walls, and the front of the stage was filled with them. In a few minutes the curtain went up, and the show started.

In the first few acts were dancing girls, and then there was a singer and a magician. Then the girls danced some more, and there was a comedian. The old man and the boys would shout wildly when the girls danced. The last act on the program, they announced, would be Vetro, the world's greatest knife thrower. They brought out a target board, and the man made several throws at it. Then a woman stood against it, and he threw knives and made an outline against her body. Then they placed the ace of a deck of cards against the target, and he said he would perform the greatest feat of all time: he would split the center of the card at forty feet. He backed off and threw, and missed the first time. Then he threw, and the knife split the center of the card. The crowd shouted and clapped, and the women stared in wonder.

When the noise stopped, the old man jumped to his feet and shouted: "Who all wants to bet that this boy here can't do that from the door here?"

It was well over a hundred feet to the door. Several men jumped up and shouted for him to sit down, and then he pulled out a roll of bills and waved them, and several men came over to cover the bet. The old man bet every cent he had on the feat.

"How much money you got, Abner?" he asked.

"I got a hundred and fifty dollars."

"Hand it here and I'll bet hit fer you," said the old man.

Pa thought long and hard about handing over their supply money, but he finally gave it to the old man. Skeeter just sat and didn't say anything.

"We got some more here," shouted the old man, and several more men came over and got in on the betting. They let the house owner hold the money. The old man had bet three hundred dollars, plus Pa's money. When the betting was all done, everyone sat down. They turned the target towards the door, and Skeeter got up and pulled out his knife.

"If'n you'll hit that shot I'll buy you enough likker sticks to last a year," said the old man.

Skeeter thought of what would happen if he did not make the throw hit the card, of what Ma would say when they came back without supplies, and how they wouldn't have any money to buy food to last during the flood. He wished the old man had kept his seat, but now there was nothing to do but go ahead.

Skeeter walked back to the door and stood for a moment. A hush swept over the crowd, and the drop of a pin could have been heard. He raised his hand, hesitated for a moment, and sent the knife flying through the air. It sailed over the end of the stage and split the card dead in the center.

The old man and Hooker boys jumped up and down and shouted as loud as they could. The crowd went wild, and Pa felt a big relief. Skeeter just went down the aisle and got his knife, came back, and sat down. The old man got the money and counted out Pa three hundred dollars, then put the rest in his pocket. When they were out of the show house, the old man bought Skeeter a big bag of likker sticks. They went to see every other show in town, and the old man paid the admissions. It was after midnight when they returned to the hotel and went to bed.

The next morning they got up and went out of the hotel to get breakfast. It was sleeting, and the wind blew against their faces. Skeeter thought of the trip home and shuddered. They went into the same restaurant they had been in the night before, and each ate a half dozen eggs and all the hot biscuits the waiter could bring out. It was a real treat for Pa and Skeeter, for they could not afford the flour to make biscuits at home, and they very seldom ate eggs. When they finished, they went back to the hotel.

"They ain't no use in us goin' back in them boats and freezin' to death while I got all this money," said the old man. "I always did have a hankerin' to ride on them steam-

boats, so let's take hit back down. We'll be home a little
after dark tonight."

"Whut about the boats?" asked Pa.

"We kin tie 'em to the side of the steamboat and pull 'em
back down. Then we kin git off at the house and save comin'
back from Mill Town."

Skeeter was thrilled at the idea of riding the steamboat.
He had always wanted to ride one.

"We'll go with you and Skeeter to buy yore supplies, and
then go on down to the docks. That boat'll leave in about a
hour."

They took their belongings, left the hotel, and went to
one of the stores for Pa to buy the supplies. Pa bought all
the food they would need, and several sides of pork, and he
bought both Ma and Theresa a new pair of shoes and a
dress, and he got himself and Skeeter each a new pair of
shoes and a new jacket. He bought Ma several bottles of
snuff, Theresa a big bag of licorice sticks, plenty of shot for
his gun, and several boxes of shells for Skeeter. They carried
the supplies down to the docks and loaded them in the
boats. The steamboat was at the dock, so the old man
bought the tickets and they went aboard.

Sun Up and Sun Down rowed the boats around to the
side of the steamboat and threw the lines up to the old man
and Pa. They tied them to the rail and the boys climbed up.
The lines were cast off from the dock, and the boat started
down the river.

They stood around the rail and watched while the boat
got under way, but the sleet was getting worse so they went
inside. The stateroom was warm, and it felt good to them, so
they started passing the jug. Before long they were all fairly
drunk and were in need of excitement.

"Let's go blow the whistle," said the old man. "I always
did want to blow one of them steamboat whistles."

They got up and went outside and climbed the ladder going to the wheelhouse. All of them carried their guns. The captain met them at the door of the wheelhouse and stopped them.

"You can't come up here," he said. "We don't allow passengers up here."

"We is here," said the old man, "and besides, we don't want to do nothin' but blow the whistle."

"We just can't allow that," said the captain.

"Well, if'n you don't mind," said the old man, "we jest goin' to do hit anyway. Now step aside if'n you don't want that little house blowed full of holes."

They shoved the captain aside and walked in the wheelhouse. The old man grabbed the whistle cord and pulled it. The whistle blew, and he shouted and pulled it again. Then he stepped aside, and the others came up one at a time and pulled the cord. One of the other passengers came up and wanted to know if the boat was in trouble, but when he saw the bearded men and the guns, he slipped back down the ladder.

When it was noon, they all went down to eat in the mess and then returned to the wheelhouse and started blowing the whistle again. The didn't stop until it was dark, and the old man knew they would soon be at the house.

"We wants to git off in a little piece," he said.

"I can't stop the boat till we get to Mill Town," said the captain. "It's against the rules."

"Well, you better jest break the rules and throw this thing in reverse," said the old man, "or I'll do hit fer you."

"I guess it'll be worth it to get rid of you," said the captain. "Both of my ears are busted now."

The captain stopped the boat, and they started down the ladder to get off. The old man turned and looked at the captain.

"Thanks fer lettin' us blow the whistle," he said, and went on down the ladder. They climbed down the lines into the boats, a deck hand cast them off, and they rowed over to the landing. The women were waiting for them at the landing.

"Whut in the world were that boat whistle cuttin' up so fer?" asked the old woman. "And whut air you all doin' gittin' off that boat?"

"Let's git out of the cold and we'll tell you all about it," said the old man. "Abner and the women air goin' to stay here tonight and go on home in the mornin'."

They walked into the house and warmed by the fire. The old man told them about the trip and about Skeeter throwing the knife and winning all the money. Pa told Ma what all he had brought and of the money he still had left. It made her very happy, and she could hardly wait to get home and try on the dress and shoes.

The women cooked supper, and the men brought out some more jugs. After supper the boys got out the fiddles and guitars and played lively music. They danced and drank and had a frolic almost as good as the one at Christmas.

SIXTEEN

THE COREY FAMILY was happy now, knowing they would not be hungry during the flood. The kitchen shelf was well stocked with meal, coffee, sugar, lard, salt, smoked sausage, and hams, and the salt pork hung from the rafters. There were ears of corn to be parched over the hearth, potatoes to be baked, and they had the crocks of fresh pork packed down in lard. Ma and Theresa tried on their new dresses and shoes many times.

There was much work to be done before the flood came. They had to bring in pine from the woods and stack it in the house, the roof had to be packed with moss, and everything they owned that floated had to be put in the house or stored on the roof. The nets and the line were brought in, and the skiff was tied to the side of the house. After they finished with the roof, they spent most of their time bringing pine from the woods. When there was no more room in the kitchen, they stacked it on the back stoop, because the pine would have to last several weeks.

One day they took their guns with them to the woods and killed a young buck. They built another smoke house in which to smoke it, and when they were finished, it was hung from the kitchen rafters with the other meats. The venison would taste good and would be a change from the pork.

When the work was finished, there wasn't much for Pa and Skeeter to do during the day, so they reset the trotline in the river. They could eat the fish until the rains came and save the other meats. When they finished running the line every morning, they spent the rest of the day hunting ducks on the bayou and along the swamp, and they went into the woods to hunt turkey. They did not bait the turkeys now but stalked them in the trees and on the ground, for one turkey was all that they could eat at a time, and they were hunting mostly to take up their time. They could have killed many bucks but did not do so. Once they killed a large buck and took it to the Hookers, for they knew that the Hookers did not have much time to hunt and would like the fresh venison. Other than that they watched the deer at their play and let them go. One night before supper Skeeter was sitting in the kitchen rigging a giant sethook and line. Ma stopped her cooking and watched him for a few minutes.

"Where in the world did you git sech a big outfit like that?" she asked.

"I got hit down at Mill Town one day," he said.

"Whut you plannin' on doin' with it?" asked Ma. "They ain't no fish big enough to swaller that thing."

"I'm goin' to ketch me a gar," said Skeeter.

"You goin' to fool around with them gar and git yoreself in another mess like you did with that big 'gator," said Ma. "You better worry 'bout ketchin' catfish and leave them big devils alone."

"How'd you like to have a good mess of gar meat fer supper tomorrow night?" asked Skeeter.

"Now you shet up sech talk as that or git out'n the kitchen," said Ma. "I ain't goin' to have you in here talkin' 'bout gar meat whiles we's fixin' supper."

"If'n you got hongry enough I bet you'd eat it," said Skeeter, "and then yore nose would grow long and turn to a sword, and yore arms would turn to fins, and you'd git scales all over you and then jump in the river, then fust things you knows you'd be eatin' raw squirrel meat and gittin' in traps."

"You shet up right this minute! You gives me the creeps talkin' like thet. Now git on out of here till I calls you." Skeeter got up and went to his room to finish rigging the line.

The next morning he went up the river and took the big hook and line with him. He selected a good, strong, willow limb that hung over the water and tied the line to it so, if he hung a gar, the limb would give and there would not be much tension on the line. If he tied it to a log or a stake or anything that would not give, the gar could easily break it. He put a whole squirrel on the giant hook and lowered it into the water and returned home.

The next morning when he went back, the willow limb was not moving, so he thought he had not made a catch. He grabbed the line to see if the bait was still on the hook, and it jerked back out of his hands. The whole willow limb shot under the water. He knew that he had something big, and it would be no use to try to pull it out of the water, so he left it and went on home. The fish would eventually wear itself out, and then he could pull it up. He didn't say anything about it when he reached home, but that afternoon he went to see if he could pull it up, and he still could not move it. The next morning it was the same way, and he left the line again. For three days he tried to pull the line up, and though he could get it up a little more each day, he could not get the fish to the top of the water.

The fourth morning he took the gaff and his rifle with him. He pulled with all his strength, and the line moved slowly upward. The point of a bill came out of the water, and before the head reached the surface, the bill was much higher than the sides of the boat. The gar shot downward and almost jerked Skeeter from the boat, but he held the line tight. When it was still for a minute, he moved the line to his left hand and grabbed the gaff and jerked it through the gar's mouth. Again he had to hold on with all his strength to keep from being pulled from the boat. When it settled down again, he held the gaff with his left hand and picked up the rifle, cocked it, and shot the gar through the head. It jumped so hard he had to let the gaff go. A thin streak of blood came to the surface, and the line was still. When he raised it this time, there was no resistance, but pulling in the dead weight was hard work. The gaff was still in its mouth so he pulled it up. When the gar finally floated up, it was almost as long as the boat and weighed at least three-hundred pounds. Skeeter thought it was the ugliest thing he had ever seen. It scared him just looking at it, so he tied the line to the rear seat and pulled the gar down the river.

When he reached the landing, he called the family out to look at it. They came down to the landing and stared at the gar floating in the water.

"How did you ever git that thing out?" asked Pa.

"Hit's been on the hook five days," said Skeeter, "and I was jest now able to git hit to the top."

"Hit scares me," said Theresa. "If'n I knowed that sech as that were runnin' aroun' in the river, I'd never even poke my hand under the water."

"Whut you goin' to do with hit?" asked Ma.

"I thought me and Pa would float hit down the river and show hit to Mr. Blanch," said Skeeter.

"Well, I'll be glad when you gits hit away from here," said Ma.

The next morning Pa and Skeeter pulled the gar down the river to Mill Town and got Mr. Blanch to come from the market and look at it. He said it was the biggest fish he had ever seen, and he didn't see how a small boy like Skeeter had landed it. It made Skeeter feel proud when he heard that, and it made Pa feel good too, for he knew that if Skeeter could land a gar that size he could do anything a man could do on the river. Mr. Blanch said he would like to have it to send away and have a trophy made of it, so they got two men to help and took it to the market. Mr. Blanch gave Skeeter a dollar and he was very happy for he did not think the gar would be worth anything. They rowed back up the river.

Each day Pa would watch the sky to see if he thought the rains were coming. Some days they had sun, but most of them were cloudy and dark. Even when the sun was out, the wind was still cold and burned their faces.

One night the wind became harder as it blew against the house, and they knew the rains would come the next day. When Pa and Skeeter went out the following morning, they had to fight against the wind to get to the boat. The marsh grass was bent flat against the ground, and moss was blowing from the cypress trees. The black clouds were flying by overhead, and there was hardly any light. The clouds were so low Skeeter thought he could reach up and touch them. When they reached the river, the rain started, and it felt like hail, as the wind blew it against their faces. It was hard to row the boat up the river. Leaves and moss and dead limbs were blowing into the water, and the wind made churning waves of water sweep down the river. When they reached the line, the rain was so heavy they could not see more than twenty feet ahead of them. They threw the fish from the line as they pulled it in, and started back down the river.

The rain was cold, and they thought they would never reach the landing. When they finally got there, they pulled the boat up the bank and tied it to the house. They brought the oars and the line inside with them. It was near noon, but it was dark as night. Limbs blew against the house, and the clouds dropped lower and lower until it looked as if they would come into the house. Great sheets of rain beat against the ground and the bayou so that even the water in the bayou was muddy.

The wind continued for another day and then stopped. The rain got harder until finally they could not see as far as the bayou. It beat against the roof and tried to come in, but Pa and Skeeter had done a good job, and the roof turned it away.

It was warm and pleasant inside. They liked the noise of the rain beating against the house, and the sleep at night was sound. Skeeter liked to lie in his bed and listen to its patter on the cypress shingles. Each did what he pleased during the day; the meals were bountiful; and at night the family sat around the hearth and parched corn and told each other tales that had been kept secret to tell during the rains. Skeeter told of the day he had seen the two bucks fight, but he never told about the night in the swamp. They sang and played games, and sometimes Pa and Ma drank too much whiskey the Hookers had given them and showed Skeeter and Theresa how they danced during their courting days.

The rain lasted for six days, and the water rose a little each day. When the water from far up the river started down, it rose much faster. When the rain had stopped, it was still cloudy and was bitterly cold outside. The water crept up the bank of the bayou and into the yard, and finally they could look out and see only a sea of muddy water. The top of the marsh grass could not be seen, and the water rose to within five feet of the floor of the house. The Coreys had many more days yet to stay in the house.

Finally the sun came out, and the water stopped rising. They could stand on the porch and see water in all directions. Logs and trash swept against the side of the house and stuck against the pilings, then went under and floated away. The water was very swift and left brown foam floating everywhere.

Then the water began to fall, dropping lower and lower each day, until finally the marsh grass could be seen, and the water was back in the banks of the bayou. They had been in the house three weeks without touching the ground.

The first day Pa and Skeeter went out they bogged up to their knees in mud, so they did not try it again for several days. In a few days the ground was dry enough to walk on. They pulled the boat and the skiff back to the landing and put the fish box back in the bayou.

There was almost as much work to be done cleaning up after the flood as there was preparing for it. Big drifts of trash and logs were all over the clearing and under the house, and it took days to clean them up. Sometimes the boat or the skiff was hit by a drifting log and had to be repaired. The pine was nearly gone, and they had to bring more from the woods. After several days the work was done, and they were ready to start fishing again.

"I shore am glad to see the bayou clear again," said Pa. "I done got me a bait of drinkin' that muddy water. Hit'll take a month to wash the mud from my belly."

"Where we goin' to set the traps, Pa?" asked Skeeter.

"Let's set 'em at the head of the bayou," he said. "They's lots of them big catfish been washed up into the swamp, and we kin ketch 'em as they start back to the river."

"We goin' to put out the line, too?" asked Skeeter.

"Tain't no use to put the line back in the river fer a while yet," said Pa. "They's still too much trash and logs washin' down it. That line would git tore up afore we got hit in the river good."

"After we gits the traps sot, let's go in the swamp giggin'," said Skeeter. "Last year after the flood I seed lots of them big catfish swimmin' aroun' in the shallow water."

"We'll give hit a try," said Pa, "but fust let's git these traps on out. You go in the house and git the stakes whiles I loads 'em in the boat."

When Skeeter came back, they got into the boat and went up the bayou. They placed the traps at the head of the bayou, facing the swamp, so they would catch all the fish that tried to get back to the river. When they returned to the house, dinner was ready, so they washed up and sat down at the table.

"You and Skeeter don't plan nothin' fer tomorrow," said Ma. "Everthing we got in this house has to be washed, and hit's jest too big a job fer me and Theresa. We better git it done whiles this weather air good, so'es you all kin jest stay here and help."

"I wasn't cut out to be no washwoman," said Pa, "but we'll stay and help jest to keep peace."

After dinner, Skeeter got out the gig, and he and Pa poled up the bayou in the skiff. Skeeter stood in the bow, and Pa handled the pole.

"Hit shore feels a lots better to be polin' aroun' the edges of the swamp knowin' that ole Steel Head ain't behind some log waitin' fer us," said Pa. "I jest couldn't feel safe knowin' that varment were runnin' aroun' loose."

"Hit do feel a mite better," said Skeeter. "Pole her aroun' that hollow log, Pa."

Pa poled the skiff alongside a hollow log that was half submerged in the water, and Skeeter lay down in the skiff and ran his hand into the log. He moved it around and around the inside of the log, and then drew it out. He had a catfish gripped by the mouth, and he held it up for Pa to see.

"Now, where in the world did you learn to do a thing like that?" asked Pa.

"Old Uncle Jobe told me that's the way they used to ketch fish all the time," said Skeeter. "He said they did hit along the rocks in the river when hit was down and caught lots of fish that way."

"You goin' to stick yore hand in the wrong thing's mouth, too. Whut if'n you reached in there and pulled out a snake?"

"They ain't no snakes out yit, and if'n they wus, he'd probably run out the other end of the log. I ain't skeered of hit, Pa."

"Well, you be careful and don't let none of them fish bite a plug out'n you. And if'n you pull out a bull 'gator and ain't got no hand left, don't come pore-mouthin' aroun' me."

"I think I seed a big 'un swimmin' aroun' over there. Pole over a little closer and let's have a look at hit."

Pa poled the skiff slowly forward, and Skeeter kept the gig raised in the air above his head. He looked around carefully and then sent the gig flying into the water. He grabbed the handle and pulled a large catfish into the skiff.

"Got him right betwix the eyes. I bet you we fill up the skiff afore we gits done."

"Well, if'n we do, we'll jest have to go to Mill Town and then fight that river back up. Them fish you hits with the gig ain't goin' to live long enough fer us to wait fer the river to slow down."

Pa poled the skiff all around the edges of the swamp, and Skeeter reached in logs and threw the gig until the skiff was loaded to capacity with fish. When it would hold no more, they started back to the bayou.

"We should uv been doin' this after the flood ever year," said Pa. "This air more fish then we kin ketch in the traps."

"Hit does do right good, don't it, Pa? I ought to take Uncle Jobe one of these fish fer givin' me that idea. He tole

me when I come back again he were goin' to tell me another
way we could ketch fish in the river jest after the flood."

"If'n we kin keep gittin' 'em like this, we may kin get
enough money to buy us stuff to make a new boat. That old
one shore ain't much longer in this world."

"I believe we kin do hit, Pa."

When they reached the landing, they strung all the fish
and put them in the box in the bayou. They washed their
hands in the bayou and went in the house for supper. It was
not ready, so they sat at the table and waited.

"I think we better put off that wash till day after tomorrow," said Pa. "Me and Skeeter done caught a plum boatload
of fish in the swamp this afternoon, and we better take 'em
to town tomorrow."

"Why can't you put that off instead?" asked Ma.

"Most of 'ems got holes in their heads and won't live. Mr.
Blanch don't like hit when the fish ain't fresh, and he's always give us more than the others cause we don't never
bring him no bad fish."

"Well, me and Theresa will jest do hit ourselves. You and
Skeeter git that washpot from under the house and build a
fire under hit afore you leaves in the mornin'. And I don't
see how you figger you'll ever git back up the river with hit
runnin' like a hound dog chasin' a fox."

"We'll stick close to the bank and make it somehow. I
shore ain't goin' to let that fish stay here and sperl. We goin'
to try to git enough spare money to build us a new boat."

"Well, jest the same you better be mouty kerful on that
river tomorrow. I ain't aimin' to be no widder woman and be
left in this swamp by myself."

"Why, purty as you air you'd have another man in no
time at all," laughed Pa.

"Now, quit makin' fun of me, afore I throw the supper
out in the back yard, and then you would come sniffin'

aroun' and talkin' to me." She had a smile on her face so Pa knew that he had not made her mad with his teasing.

"I were jest tryin' to tell you how purty you are, and don't worry about bein' no widder woman, 'cause I ain't got no hankerin' to be gar bait on the bottom of that muddy river."

After breakfast was done the next morning, Pa and Skeeter brought the big iron washpot from under the house and filled it with water. They built a fire under it for the water to boil, then tied a rope from the back stoop to a tree to use for a line to hang the clothes on when the washing was done. They put the mattresses out to sun and brought all the quilts and clothes out to the washpot. When this was done, they loaded the boat to leave.

They did not mind getting a late start, for Pa was afraid of being on the river before daylight. The river was most dangerous just after the flood. The current was swift and treacherous, and big logs raced down the middle. Whirlpools would suck logs under, and then send them shooting back into the air. If one hit a boat, it would smash it to pieces. They stopped the boat at the mouth of the bayou and watched the boiling muddy water race by in front of them.

"I almost hates to go out in hit," said Pa. "Hold on to yore backbone when we hits that current, and if'n you see a log go under, head fer the bank as quick as you kin, and fer gosh sakes don't let the boat git sideways, or we'll be gone fer shore."

"I think I kin handle my side if'n you kin handle yores," said Skeeter.

They slowly rowed the boat into the river, and when the current caught it, the boat shot downstream like a bullet. The water boiled and splashed around it, and Pa and Skeeter fought to keep the bow pointed downstream.

"Even the Hookers ain't never gone this fast," shouted Pa. "I believe she's goin' to take to the air and fly."

The trees seemed to fly by as the boat sped along with the current. The water was filled with trash, logs, and the dead bodies of small animals, all engrossed in a mad race down the river. When Pa and Skeeter came to curves in the river, they had to fight with the oars to keep the boat from being smashed into the bank. Big whirlpools were around the edges, and the water boiled and bubbled around them. Bits of trash would go around and around in them and then disappear beneath the surface. Pa kept glancing back to keep a watch for logs. He saw a big one hit a whirlpool, spin around, and then disappear.

"Let's fight her into the bank quick!" he shouted. "They's a log comin'!"

They pulled with the oars and maneuvered the boat close to the bank. Limbs were hanging just over the water, and they had to lie down sometimes to keep from being knocked from the boat. They looked down the river and saw the log shoot out of the muddy water and sail high into the air. It came down with a splash and raced on in front of them.

"What will happen if'n one of them logs were to come up under a steamboat like that?" asked Skeeter.

"I guess hit would go right up through the smokestack," said Pa. "I shore wouldn't want to ride one of them boats with the river like this."

They pulled the boat back into the middle of the river, and the docks at Mill Town came into sight.

"Whut we goin' to do now?" asked Skeeter. "If'n we head her into them docks goin' like this we'll take docks and all on down the river with us."

"I don't know jest exactly whut to do," said Pa, "but we shore got to do somethin' quick or we'll be past Mill Town afore we sees hit good."

"Why don't we turn around in the boat and row back the other way, Pa? Maybe that'll slow her down a mite."

"I guess that's 'bout the only thing we kin do."

They turned around and started pulling the oars as hard as they could. It slowed the boat down a little but not enough. They steered it out of the current, and it headed straight for the docks. They pulled the oars with all their might, but they couldn't stop the movement of the boat. It was nearing the end of the docks.

"You stand up and grab one of the pilings and hold on," shouted Pa, "and I'll try to throw the rope over hit."

When the boat reached the end of the docks, Skeeter grabbed one of the pilings and hooked his feet to the side of the boat. He thought his body would break in two. The boat swung around, but before Pa could throw the line over the piling, Skeeter's feet slipped and he was left dangling on the piling. The boat swung around and hit the bank, and stuck against a tree in the water. Pa jumped out, tied the line to another tree, and raced back up the bank to the dock. He pulled Skeeter up from the piling, and they both went down and pulled the boat along the bank to the dock. Then they tied it up.

"That's the dernest landin' I ever seed made," said Pa. "I shore don't want to do that again."

"I ain't got no hankerin' to try hit again neither."

They got the fish out of the boat and started to the market, and Skeeter kept one to give Uncle Jobe.

"You run on down there and take him that fish whiles these air bein' weighed, and then hurry on back," said Pa. "We got to start back jest as soon as I gets paid, 'cause hit's goin' to be somethin' tryin' to git back up that river."

"Ain't you goin' to buy any supplies?" asked Skeeter.

"We still got enough at home without buyin' none today," said Pa. "And hit'll be all we kin do to pull ourselves back without tryin' to take any supplies."

THE RIVER IS HOME   183

They took the fish to the market and Skeeter ran down the lane to Uncle Jobe's. They greeted each other, and Skeeter handed him the fish.

"I brought you a catfish to et," said Skeeter. "I done like you tole me about them logs and got a bunch of 'em."

"I knowed you would," said Uncle Jobe. "I'm goin' to give you somethin' else to git 'em with, too."

He got up and went into the shack and returned with a paper bag in his hand. He handed it to Skeeter and then sat back down.

"Now you do jest like I tells you and you'll git plenty," he said. "Git you a gallon jug and pour this stuff in hit. Don't put no top on hit, neither. Then tie a short piece of rope to the top of the jug, and git you a weight and tie to it. Find you a place in the river where they's a cove and the water ain't runnin' swift, and throw this in. Jest git back a ways and hit will do the rest."

"I shore thanks you," said Skeeter. "Me and Pa air tryin' to git enough extra fish to git up the money to build a new boat."

"Well, you air sho' welcome, and jest bring me another cat next time you comes. I sho' like them cats when they air fried good and brown."

Skeeter skipped back up the lane with the bag. Pa was waiting for him in front of the market.

"Whut's that you got in that bag?" asked Pa.

"Hit's somethin' Uncle Jobe give me to catch us some more extra fish. I'll show you how hit works when we gits the chance."

They went back to the dock and got into the boat. Skeeter untied the line, and they started the trip home. Several times they didn't think they would make it. They had to stay close to the bank and row hard to move the boat forward. Many times they grabbed limbs and held the boat so they could stop and rest. The current shoved them back every time their oars came out of the water, and the boat moved forward only a little more than it moved back each time. It took them the rest of the morning and all afternoon to reach the mouth of the bayou, and when they finally reached the landing, they had to sit and rest before they could get out of the boat. Their arms and backs ached worse than they had ever done before. They went into the house and went to bed without eating any supper.

"Never thought I'd see the day when you two would go to bed without eatin' no supper," Ma said, the next morning. "That river must have really been somethin' to git you that way."

"Hit were like tryin' to tow one of them steamboats up stream with a paddle," said Pa. "I ain't got no hankerin' to try that again afore the river slows up a mite."

Pa and Skeeter didn't gig any more fish, but they caught so many in the traps that the fish box wouldn't hold any more. The river didn't go down any, and the current stayed just as swift, so they finally had to make another trip to town and fight the river as they had before.

"Hit looks like we mout as well git used to fightin' the river and go on abouts our business," said Pa, "cause hit don't look like it's goin' to slow down fer a while yet. They must have been a powerful lot of water som-ers fer hit to keep comin' like this."

"Why don't we go up to West Cut and try this stuff Uncle Jobe give me?" asked Skeeter. "Today would be a good day fer hit."

"I guess hit suits me," said Pa. "If'n we keeps gettin' the fish likes we is now we'll shore have that new boat afore long."

"We'll need one of them empty whiskey jugs, a piece of rope and a weight," said Skeeter. "You git the jug, and I'll git the rest."

This was the first time they had been to West Cut since the flood, and the cove had been washed out and was much bigger than it was before. The water in the cove was not swift, and now it hardly moved at all. When they had pulled the boat to the bank, Skeeter started doing what Uncle Jobe had told him to do.

"Let me look at that stuff," said Pa. Skeeter handed him the bag and he examined it and handed it back to Skeeter. "Hit looks like some kind of lime."

Skeeter poured it into the jug and tied the rope to the weight and mouth of the jug.

"He said to jest throw it in the water and git out'n the way," said Skeeter.

"I don't see whut hit kin do to ketch fish," said Pa. "Maybe the fish air supposed to eat the stuff as it comes out'n the jug and git sick. But I'd shore hate to have to sit here and wait that long."

"Well, I mout as well throw hit in and see whut happens. Push her out in the middle."

Pa pushed the boat out in the cove and Skeeter threw the jug into the water. The weight pulled it down, and it sank from sight. Pa rowed the boat back out of the way.

"I ain't seed nothin' happen," said Pa.

"Maybe hit ain't had time yit," said Skeeter. "They's bubbles comin' up now."

They sat for a few seconds watching the water, and then a muffled explosion went off deep below them. A geyser of water shot into the air and poured down on them. The boat rocked and nearly threw them into the river.

"Whut in the hell air that nigger tryin' to do!" shouted Pa. "He done dern near got us kilt, and I ain't seed no fish yit!"

"Look at that!" shouted Skeeter, and pointed to the middle of the cove.

Dozens of fish were rising to the surface and floating around in the water. There were big ones, little ones, and they kept coming up until the water was filled with fish.

"Well, I'll be derned," said Pa. "I wouldn't believe it if'n I weren't seeing hit with my own eyes. Let's git busy."

They rowed the boat around and scooped the fish out of the water with their hands. When they were through, the boat was loaded with fish.

"Whut you think of hit now?" asked Skeeter. "Old Uncle Jobe shore do know a lot of things, don't he?"

"I's powerful glad to git all these fish," said Pa, "but I'll be dogged if'n we air ever goin' to do that again. We could have got blowed slam out'n the boat foolin' with that stuff, whutever hit were. You jest thank Uncle Jobe, but don't take none uv that stuff no more."

They made one more trip down the raging river, and then the current began to slow down. The water dropped a little each day, and finally it was back down to normal. The trips to town were not so hard now, and they went every Saturday and brought back supplies. Each time they had a little money left and put it with their other savings. They put the line back into the river, and the fishing stayed good. The Coreys were beginning to prosper a little.

"If'n this keeps up we'll have enough money to git the boat and maybe enough to tide us through the low water this summer," said Pa. "Hit shore would please me if'n I didn't have to work at the mill this summer. Maybe me and Skeeter would have enough time to clear enough land to have a big corn crop, and we could stop havin' to buy so much meal."

"Hit would shore be nice," said Ma, "and maybe the Lord will be good to us, and hit will be that way."

"I shore hope He is," said Pa. "I shore hope He is."

SEVENTEEN

IT WAS NOT LONG before all traces of the flood were gone. The wind blew the drifts of trash and leaves from along the river banks, and the sun dried out the low places of ground. Buzzards flew along the bank in search of the dead animals, and when found, devoured them. The winds still blew, and sometimes it was cold, but the days were more sunny than cloudy. When they had rain, it was gentle, and the sun was setting later in the west.

One day Skeeter found a group of small, blue violets growing in the clearing, and a few days later he saw a robin, and he knew spring had come again. It could be felt in the air, on the river, and even the trees seemed to sense it and sway in anticipation of the new coat of leaves they would get. The marsh grass was turning green again, and the ducks were flying away to the north. The trees were covered with small buds. The sky was filled with great white clouds, mixed with patches of deep blue, and the sun was beginning to feel warm and pleasant. The thick wool jacket was not comfortable during the day, the shoes would soon come off, and the water of the bayou would soon be warm enough to swim in.

Each day the tiny buds on the trees grew; the snakes and turtles came out to sun themselves on logs; and the grass turned greener. The squirrels came out early in the morning, played in the trees all day, and the baby frogs began to bellow in the swamp at night. The katydids chirped at sundown, and the fireflies filled the night with thousands of small diamonds sparkling in the darkness. The tiny buds of the trees grew until they burst, and everything was splashed with green. Spring had arrived with all her glory, and the river was beautiful again.

Gone were the bare limbs that raised themselves in solemn submission to the black clouds of the sky, and gone were the cold winds and rains that burned the face and chilled the spirits. The minnows swam in the bayou, the birds sang to the air, the animals rejoiced that the dark days were behind, and the sky was filled with light.

The clean, black ground of the garden was broken into rows, and the seeds were covered with the cool soil. The sun would warm them, the gentle rains would quench their thirst, the rich black soil would nourish them, and they would burst from the ground in appreciation of spring. It was a wonderful time for the birds of the air, the animals of the woods, the reptiles of the swamp, the plants of the ground, the humans of the clearing. All were glad to be alive, and they drank of the sun and air until they were drunk with the intoxication of spring.

The trips to town were pleasant again. The trees and vines were beautiful, and Pa and Skeeter could see the small animals at play. Birds sang to them, crows shouted at them, squirrels talked to them, and the turtles paid no heed to them. Everything looked different, except the water of the river; it kept its muddy color even though all else had changed. There could be sun, or rain, or it could be winter or spring, but the brown water of the river stayed the same. If it was low, or if it was raging across the marsh flats and into the clearing, it made no difference. It paid no heed to what was going on around it; it was unchangeable in its ways. It seemed that God made it to be muddy, and muddy it would be, regardless of what came or went, of what traveled up and down its far reaches.

The days rolled on, and the fishing stayed good, and sometimes Pa and Skeeter had to make two trips to town a week to sell the fish. This turn of good fortune made the family happy, and there were no flashes of temper or ill feelings among them. The days seemed more sunny than ever, and the sky seemed bluer than they had ever known it. Finally Pa decided that the savings were enough for the new boat and to keep him at the clearing all summer, so one morning they rowed up to the Hookers to see about the supplies to do the building. The old man saw them coming and met them at the landing. They exchanged greetings and went to the house.

"You ain't goin' to Fort Henry ary time soon, air you?" asked Pa.

"Why shore," said the old man. "We's goin' the fust of the week. Hit's the fust time we been up this spring, and we got a big load to run up. Air they somethin' we could git fer you?"

"Yes," said Pa, "if'n you don't mind. The fishin' has been good, so me and Skeeter has saved up enough to git the stuff to build us a new boat. That old one air jest about shot, and we wants one that air bigger and kin haul more stuff. I knowed you was mighty good on buyin', and you knows more about buildin' boats than ary man abouts here, so I'd shore appreciate hit if'n you would git the stuff fer me."

"I'll shore be glad to do hit, Abner," he said. "I'll git the best stuff I kin find, so'es you will have as good a boat as ary man on the river. When we gits back, me and the boys will build hit up to the house and bring hit down to you. We kin git it done in a day."

"That'd be mighty nice," said Pa, "but we shore willin' to help with the buildin'. We ain't askin' fer you to do it all."

"I know you ain't," said the old man, "but we'd right well enjoy hit, and then it would be a good surprise fer you when you first sees hit."

"Well, they's one more thing," said Pa. "Skeeter here wants the boat painted, so git enough paint to do hit and one of them breshes to put it on with."

"Whut color you want?" asked the old man.

"Red," said Skeeter.

"Then red it will be," said the old man. "That'll shore make a purty-lookin' boat."

Pa gave the old man the money, and they went back down the river. They were both excited the rest of the week and could hardly wait until the Hookers got the material and finished the boat. They did not even enjoy their Saturday trip to Mill Town for thinking about the boat. It was the only thing on their minds, and they could have no peace until they saw the finished boat. Ma and Theresa were excited, too, but not as much as Pa and Skeeter.

One morning, the first of the week, Pa was at the landing and saw a boat with three men in it coming up the bayou, and he watched as it came toward the landing. The men were dressed in fancy hunting clothes and carried guns, so Pa knew they were not swamp folks. When they got closer, he recognized them as the three Smith brothers and could see that they were drunk and had several empty jugs in their boat. They pulled the boat to the landing and walked up the bank, one of them bringing his gun.

"Howdy," said Pa. "Glad to see you fellers done got friendly and come a callin'. Come on in and sit a spell."

"Shet yore goddam mouth," said one of the brothers. "We ain't come callin' on no low son of a bitch like you. You got whiskey to sell?"

"I shore ain't," said Pa. "I don't make no whiskey; I jest fish."

"He's lyin'!" said one of the men. "All these damned swamp rats lie like that."

"I ain't tellin' no lie," said Pa, "and I ain't wantin' no trouble from you fellers. I jest ain't got no whiskey, but if'n I did, you'd be welcome to hit. You kin git some 'bout five mile up the river, if you wants to go there."

"We want it now," said the brother. "He's lyin'. Hold the gun on him, and I'll go look in his house."

The brother with the gun pointed the barrel at Pa, while one of the others staggered to the house. He climbed the back steps and went in.

"Don't make a move," said the one with the gun. "I been wantin' to kill me a swamp rat, and I'd jest as soon blow yore brains all over this bayou."

Pa did not move, and then he heard Theresa scream. He turned and saw the man shove Ma down the back steps and drag Theresa by her arm across the yard. He shoved Ma ahead of them.

"I didn't find no whiskey, but look what I did find," he said. "I didn't know they was anything that looked like this hid out in these swamps."

"She sure is a beauty," said the one with the gun. "What you got in mind?"

"Well, if we can't have any whiskey, we can sure have some fun," he said. "You hold the gun on these two, and I'll take her first. Then I'll come back and you all can have her."

He started dragging Theresa towards some bushes up the bayou, but she fought back, and he was having a hard time.

"She sure is a little wildcat, ain't she?" he said.

"You jest don't know how to handle these swamp rats," said the one with the gun. "Hold her arms and I'll show you how to quiet her down."

The brother pinned both of Theresa's arms behind her, while the one with the gun walked over to them. He drew back the gun and hit her hard behind the head with the butt. She slumped to the ground and blood trickled down her neck. Then he came back and held the gun on Ma and Pa. "She won't give you no trouble now," he said.

None of them had seen the figure of the small boy crawling across the clearing towards them. Skeeter had seen the man hit Theresa with the gun, and he was creeping silently into range. When he saw the man start dragging Theresa's limp body into the bushes, he pulled his knife from his belt and drew it back. The blade spun through the air and struck the man with the gun. He slumped to his knees, screamed and fell to the ground. The gun went off, and Pa staggered backward. When Skeeter saw what had happened, he sat down and started retching violently. The other two brothers ran to the boat for their guns. Ma ran to where Theresa was lying.

In the excitement none of them had seen the two boat-loads of men silently towing a new red boat up the bayou and pulling into the landing. As the brothers stumbled down the bank, the Hooker boys trained their guns on them.

"Now jest git on back up there," said the old man, "till we finds out what this air all abouts."

The two men retreated up the bank with the Hookers behind them. Pa had risen to his feet and came towards them. Skeeter was still sitting on the ground retching.

"Whut air all this?" asked the old man. "Whut's these low bred sons of bitches doin' here?"

"They were tryin' to ruin Theresa," said Pa, "but Skeeter planted his knife in that one there. When he fell, he shot me in the shoulder. They knocked Theresa in the head with the gun, and she's over there in the bushes."

When he heard this, Sparky ran to the bushes and picked Theresa up in his arms. Her red hair was stained even redder with blood, and she was unconscious.

"Git her on in the house so'es her ma kin see 'bout her," said the old man. "A couple of you boys git some rope and tie these bastards up. Sun Up, you git a fire started and boil some water so'es we kin treat Abner's wound. How bad air hit, Abner?"

"Hit ain't too bad," said Pa. "Jest knicked me a little mite in the shoulder."

Two of the boys returned with the rope and bound the two men's hands and feet.

"We'll git the law on you sons of bitches," said one of the brothers.

"You fellers better be makin' yore peace with the Lord, 'stead of studyin' 'bout the law," said the old man.

Sparky took Theresa into the house, put her on a bed, and Ma came in and bathed her face with a wet cloth. She opened her eyes and looked up at Sparky. "Oh, Sparky," she said, "I'm so sorry this had to happen."

"Hit's all right," said Sparky, "hit ain't none of yore fault."

"Don't leave me, Sparky," she said. "Please don't leave me."

He bent down and kissed her on the lips and laid his head on her shoulder. Ma came back into the room with a bucket of water and a clean cloth. "Hold her hands while I bathe that wound," she said.

Sparky kissed her again and held her hands in his. He could feel her grip tighten as Ma touched the wet cloth to the deep cut.

The old man walked over and lifted Skeeter from the ground. Skeeter was still retching and crying bitterly. "I done kilt a man," he sobbed. "I ain't never thought I would kill a man."

"Don't you fret none," said the old man, "cause you done the right thing, Skeeter. You done right in the sight of the Lord, so don't worry 'bout hit. We all right proud of you."

He led Skeeter to the bayou and bathed his face in the cool water, then led him to the back of the house. They had taken Pa's shirt off, and the old man examined the wound. "Tain't too bad," he said, "we'll have it fixed up in a little. It jest might be sore fer a day or so."

When he had finished with Pa, the old man started into the house to see how Theresa was doing. As he entered the kitchen, Sparky was walking from the room.

"How air she?" he asked.

"She got a pretty bad cut," said Sparky, "but she's goin' to be O.K."

"Well, you go back in the room and stay with her and help her ma," said the old man.

Sparky started towards the back door. "I'm goin' out in the back where them two . . . "

"Goddammit!" shouted the old man. "You do like I tole you! I'm goin' to handle them two out there, so'es you git back in that room."

The old man walked out the back door and over to where the two brothers were lying. "Everybody come on over here," he shouted. Pa and all the Hooker boys came over to him.

"Whut we goin' to do?" asked Pa. "We goin' to turn 'em over to the law in Fort Henry?"

"Tain't no use in that," said the old man. "They'd jest git some of them slick lawyers and come down here and hang Skeeter from a cypress tree. We'll have the trial right here. I'll be the jedge, and you all be the jury."

"The law will git you if you mess with us," said one of the brothers.

"Tain't no law on this part of the river but the law of right and wrong," said the old man, "and you two bastards oughta know which is which."

The old man turned to the others and spoke: "Men, you know whut the charges is again these two. They has tried to ruin a innocent young girl and could have ruint the happiness of two young children and broke the hearts of two families. They also would have committed murder if'n we hadn't come up. Do ary one of you say they ain't guilty?" No one spoke or raised a hand. "Then I commits them to the muddy water of the river, and may the Lord have mercy on their damned souls."

The two brothers didn't say anything for they didn't believe what was happening. They thought the men were only trying to scare them.

"We better not do that," said Pa. "Whut we goin' to do if'n the law comes around here lookin' fer 'em?"

"Damn the law!" shouted the old man. "The law wouldn't do a damn thing but turn these bastards loose and hang Skeeter. We'll put guns in their boat and turn the boat loose in the river. With all them empty whiskey jugs in there folks will think they jest got drunk and fell in the river. Besides, the law can't see to the bottom of that muddy river, if the law even comes." The old man turned and faced his sons. "Sun Up," he said, "git them sons of bitches on out of my sight, and when you gits done, turn the boat loose on the river." He turned and walked into the house, and Pa followed him.

Sun Up looked under the house and found three heavy trotline weights and tied them to the men. They loaded them in the boat and rowed to the river. Sun Up lifted one of them from the boat and lowered him until only his head was above water. "Got any last words to say?" he asked.

When the man started to speak, Sun Up released his grip, and only bubbles came to the surface of the muddy water.

When the other brother saw this he fainted, and they threw his body and the dead one into the water. Bubbles rose to the surface for a few minutes, then the water flowed as usual. They returned to the house, towed the brothers' boat to the river and turned it loose, then went back to the landing. Pa and the old man came out of the house as they returned, and Skeeter walked to the landing with them. He had stopped crying and didn't look as scared as he had.

"In all this excitement you ain't even seed yore new boat, Abner," said the old man. Pa looked down the landing at the sleek new red boat.

"Hit shore air a beauty," said Pa. "Hit gives my pore old soul a thrill jest to stand and look at it. I never thought I'd be goin' to town in somethin' that looked as purty as that."

"Hit may leak a little at first," said the old man, "but jest as soon as hit's been in the water long enough hit's goin' to start swellin', and them cracks will seal up so tight you can't even git a gnat's eyeball through 'em."

"I can hardly wait to try it out," said Pa.

"I know jest how you feels," said the old man. "We was jest like that when we built our new ones. I brought a little mite of white paint in case you wants to name hit. A purty boat like that ought to have a name."

"I guess hit do at that," said Pa. "Whut you wants to call it, Skeeter?"

"Let's name it Steel Head," said Skeeter. "If'n hits as tough as that critter were, it'll shore be a good one."

"'I think that suits hit real well," said Pa. "Kin ary one of you fellows write?"

"Can't none of us do it," said the old man.

"Me and Skeeter can't do it either," said Pa, "but Theresa kin, so soon as she gits over that lick on the head we'll git her to do hit fer us."

"We better git on back up the river, boys," said the old man. "One of you run to the house and git Sparky." One of the boys ran to the house, and Sparky returned with him. They all got into their boats, and the old man turned to Pa. "Abner," he said, "we shore sorry this had to happen, but I guess hit would have come sooner or later. Them bastards was rotten through and through. The best thing is that we all forgets it ever happened. Let's don't none of us ever say another word about hit."

"I guess that suits me fine," said Pa.

"Well, you and yore folks come up to the house Sunday and we'll have dinner and celebrate yore new boat," said the old man.

"We'll shore be proud to be there," said Pa.

The Hookers pushed away from the landing and rowed down the bayou. Pa and Skeeter watched them until they turned into the river and disappeared from sight.

EIGHTEEN

THE COREYS left early Sunday morning for the Hookers' with everyone dressed in his best. Pa's shoulder was sore but not too sore to row, and Theresa felt good though she wore a large bandage on her head. Ma and Theresa had on the new dresses Pa had brought them from Fort Henry before the flood. Ma had made herself a jar of sassafras tea to take along, for she didn't feel very good that morning. The trip up was very pleasant, and the rowing was a joy instead of a hardship to Pa and Skeeter, for the new boat skimmed the surface of the water with the grace of a swan. It was a beautiful day, and the air was filled with the clean, sweet smell of late spring. Flowers of all colors were growing along the banks, and the wistaria vines in the trees had burst into bloom, dotting the green of the trees with their purple. Dogwood trees were white with their blooms, and the honeysuckle blended in with its pink and red. The buds of the magnolia had opened, and the women thrilled to the beauty of the great white flowers. Pa and Skeeter were not so aware of this beauty as were Ma and Theresa.

After they arrived at the Hookers' landing and exchanged greetings, they sat on the front porch to talk, with no mention being made of what had happened to the Smith brothers. The old woman admired the new dresses that Ma and Theresa wore, and the men talked of nothing but the new boat and what a pleasure it was to use it. All the men went down to the landing and took turns rowing it on the river. They were so interested in the boat that they forgot to pass the jugs around before the noon meal, and when they got back to the house, the food was already on the table. When the meal was finished, the men went to the porch to make up for the time they had lost on the jugs, and the women cleaned the table. When the work was finished, Ma lay down on a bed to rest for she still wasn't feeling any better. After she rested, she went to the porch to join in the talk. The boys and Skeeter had gone to the still, and Sparky and Theresa were down at the giant tree, so it was quiet and peaceful, and Ma felt a little better.

"I shore am glad you folks has been blessed with goodness lately," said the old man. "Hit's about time you got some of good 'stead of the bad."

"Hit pleases us well, too," said Pa, "and we're mighty thankful fer it. I always said that sooner or later times would git a mite better fer us, cause we's always minded our own business and let the other feller be. I believe that if'n a man tries to do right, and don't give trouble to other folks, the Lord will look out fer him and show him some of the goodness."

"You air shore right," said the old man. "They would never be no trouble on this river if'n folks would jest learn to stop messin' with other people and treat each other as the Lord intended for them to do. They ain't no cause fer them town people and them boatmen to come through here actin' high and mighty like they was the only ones on the river fit to live."

"That don't matter too much to me," said Pa. "Hit don't make me no mind what they think of me and my family jest so long as they let us be and the Lord keeps on givin' us a little goodness."

"Well, hit matters to me," said the old man. "If'n them fellers come aroun' here puttin' out trouble, they'll git more than they bargained fer."

Skeeter came around the side of the house, climbed the steps, and sat on the floor by the old man. "Has you ever seed the big river?" he asked.

"You mean the Mississippi?" said the old man.

"Yeah, that's hit," said Skeeter.

"I seed hit when I were a young buck 'bout like Jeff air."

"I heard niggers talkin' 'bout hit down to Mill Town one day, and I been wantin' to git somebody to tell me 'bout hit whut had been there."

"You git on out of here and play with them boys and quit worryin' Mr. Hooker with all them questions," said Ma.

"Let him stay," said the old man. "I don't mind tellin' him 'bout hit."

Skeeter was glad that the old man had said he could stay, and he settled back against a porch post to listen. The old man looked at him and started talking.

"When I were a young buck, I come from a family as big as this'n I got now, and hit were all boys, too. We lived over in Hancock County on the Wolf River and made whiskey jest like we do here now. Ever once in a while my pa would git the hankerin' fer killin', and he'd git all his boys together and head fer the woods. He always said that when he got that way, he'd 'truther go to the woods and kill the animals then stay around and shoot up some white folks or niggers. We'd take to the woods and stay fer three or four days, sometimes a week, and kill ary thing that walked on four feet, and then go on back home when he were satisfied. Sometimes we'd go clear over to the Pascagoula River and come back along Red Creek."

"Did you see ary bears?" asked Skeeter.

"We seed plenty," said the old man, "and killed plenty, too.

"Then one year my ma died, and pa took the killin' spells soon after that. He made us board up the house, put ever-thing away, and told us that we mout be gone a long time. He said we was goin' slam to the big river and back. That suited us boys jest fine, cause we wanted to see hit, too. We struck out afoot north till we hit the Black River and then followed hit to where hit started from. We made camps all along the way and et the game we killed. We kept headin' north, and soon came to the Strong River and camped there fer a couple of days. That were one of the purtiest little riv-ers we seed. Hit were full of rocks and falls, and they were plenty of game along it. We moved on till we hit this muddy Pearl and made a camp on the top of Le Fleur's bluff. The next day we walked right down the streets of Jackson, whis-key jugs, hound dogs, and all. Them people shore thought we was a sight.

"All that country up in there were mighty purty. They were long rollin' hills, and big pines, and they wasn't much swamp. We cut straight across from Jackson, and crossed the Big Black, and then come out on the Mississippi down from Vicksburg. We threwed up a camp and killed deer and stayed there till Pa was tired of lookin' at that big river."

"Were they ary steamboat on hit like they air here?" asked Skeeter.

"We seed steamboats on hit what would make the ones here look like rowboats," said the old man. "Hit nigh on scared Pa to death furst time we seed one of them big bug-gers churnin' up the river.

"After we camped there fer a spell, we headed south and left the river. We cut back in and camped along Bayou

Pierre fer a while. They were the biggest bluffs and hills through that country that I ever seed, and we most near broke our necks fallin' over 'em. When we left there, we went on down and camped along the Homochitto River, and then went on down into Louisiana. We hit the Amite River and followed it until hit met the Blind, and then went slam on down to Lake Maurepas. The country were gittin' full of marsh and swamp, and the skeeters were powerful bad, so we cut north and went aroun' the lake. We run into the top of Lake Pontchartrain, and I'll never fergit the look on Pa's face when he took a drink and found out that that water were salt. That salt water give Pa a bellyful, so we cut back towards home. We crossed the Tangiapahoa, the Tchefuncta and Bayou Chitto and then run back into the Pearl. We headed down through the marsh country and come out at Saint Louis Bay, and follered it around to where the Wolf ran into it. Then we went back up the Wolf to home. Hit took us nigh on three months to make that trip, and when we got back, somebody had done stole our whiskey still. Pa went on a rampage and got hisself shot by one of the Cajuns, and I come here to live."

"You've jest about seed everthing, ain't you?" asked Skeeter. "But how did you all know all them rivers when you come to them?"

"Hit weren't like it air here," he said. "They was a lot of people livin' all along up there, and lots of towns, and the people would tell us where we was. We didn't have to ask nobody when we hit the Mississippi though. We knowed whut hit were when we first seed it. Hit were the widest piece of river I ever seed."

"I shore wish I could see it and go aroun' like you did," said Skeeter.

"I been thinkin' 'bout gittin' the boys and makin' a trip like that sometimes, and if'n we goes, you kin shore go along with us."

"Well, right now we better make us a trip down the Pearl to home," said Ma. "I ain't feelin' a mite too good, and I better git home and lie on the bed."

Pa sent Skeeter to get Theresa, and he and Ma went down to the boat with the old man and woman following.

"I shore hope you ain't gittin' sick," said the old woman. "Hit would be mouty bad to have to lie in the house all the time with this purty weather we air havin'."

"I think I'll be all right after a good rest tonight," said Ma. "Hit ain't really nothin' mouch to worry 'bout."

In a few minutes Skeeter came down, and Theresa returned. They said good-by to the old man and woman and started down the river. The sun had sunk low in the west, and the shadows of the tall trees made dark avenues across the water. As Pa and Skeeter sent the boat skimming along, small circles of brown foam trailed behind them. It was not long before they were at the landing.

Ma drank some more hot tea and went to bed. Theresa fixed the supper for Pa and Skeeter, and they helped her clean up when they were finished. They sat on the porch until the moon came up behind the cypress trees casting its silver up the bayou, and then they went to bed.

Ma was not up the next morning when Pa and Skeeter left to run the traps and line. Theresa fixed their breakfast, and they let Ma sleep. When they returned, she was still in the bed. Her face was red, and she had quilts piled on top of her. Pa went into the room and felt of her face.

"Don't you feel any better yit?" he asked. "If'n you don't I'll fix you some more tea."

"I think that might help a little," she said. "I guess I'll be all right in a while."

Pa fixed her the tea and she drank it, but at noon she couldn't eat any food. They let her sleep most of the day, but when she awoke she was much worse. Her head burned like fire, and she could not lift herself from the bed. They sat up with her most of the night, and she finally fell asleep.

Pa and Skeeter were on the way to Mill Town at dawn the next morning to bring the doctor back to look at Ma. They were afraid and didn't know what to do, for they had never seen her sick like this before. When they reached the docks, they went straight to the doctor's house and persuaded him to go back with them. It was the middle of the morning when they got back to the house, and Ma was much worse. The doctor went into the room with her and told them to stay outside.

It seemed to Pa that the doctor had been in the room for hours. Finally he came back to the kitchen.

"What air hit, doctor?" asked Pa. "Air she very sick?"

"She's a very sick woman," said the doctor. "She's got a bad case of the fever, and if she doesn't get the proper care, she'll probably die. I think I can get a nurse to come up here and stay if you have the money, but if you haven't, you may as well start diggin' the grave."

"I got the money," said Pa.

"Well, let's get on back down the river as soon as possible so I can send the nurse up here with the proper medicine before the woman dies."

The doctor sat in the rear of the boat, and they started back down the river. They paid no heed to anything but the speed they could get out of the boat. Skeeter looked hard at the doctor seated before him. He was not such an old man, but his face was wrinkled as with age. He wore a beard on his chin, and an old black hat covered his thin, gray hair. His small, black eyes had a far-away and vague look in them, as if he had seen much of the world and was weary of it all. Skeeter hated him, and the hatred stood out in the way he tightened his mouth as he looked at the doctor. He blamed this man, this stranger, for what had happened. The man had no right to come in their house and say that his mother might die. Things had always been all right before this man came, and he should have stayed away. It was the first real hate Skeeter had ever known, and when the doctor saw the look in Skeeter's eyes, he would not look at him again. Skeeter had not hated even Steel Head like this.

When they reached the docks, they went back to the doctor's house. He told them he would go see the woman and that it would probably be a while before she could get her things to leave. He asked Pa for money to get medicine, and Pa gave him half the savings that he had. They waited at the house, while the doctor went for the woman. It seemed to them that he would never return and that Ma would surely die before they could get back, but finally the doctor did return. The woman had a small, black bag with her, so Pa took the bag and they went back to the boat.

Skeeter studied this woman on the trip back just as he had studied the doctor, and he hated her just as much. She had no right to be going to their house, but if it would help Ma, he would not complain. The woman was fat like Ma, and middle aged, and her face was wrinkled like the doctor's. Her hair was gray and unkempt, and her eyes had a hard and unsympathetic look in them.

When they reached home, the woman took the bag and went straight to the bed. She wouldn't let anyone come into the room, so they sat around the back stoop. She stayed in the room the rest of the day and came out only a few minutes to eat supper. When darkness came, she took a candle from the bag, so she could have light in the room. She lit it over the hearth and returned.

Pa got a quilt so he and Skeeter could sleep on the kitchen floor and let the woman stay in Skeeter's bed, but the woman did not go to sleep or come out of the room. Pa, Skeeter, and Theresa sat in the kitchen and stared into space. They did not talk, and they did not seem to see each other, but they were all thinking the same thing. They sat up that night until they fell asleep on the floor, and when they awoke at daylight, the woman was still in the room, and the bed had not been touched. About the middle of the morning she came out and asked for coffee.

"How air she now?" asked Pa.

"She's passed over the worse," said the woman. "She's not goin' to die, but she's still bad sick. It'll be a long time before she's well again."

"Well, thank God she's goin' to live," said Pa.

"She's asleep now," said the woman, "so don't any of you go in the room. I'm goin' to sleep some myself, so please wake me just after noon."

Pa sat at the table and buried his face in his hands. Theresa sat beside him, but Skeeter got up and went into the yard. He felt better now that he knew Ma would live. He did not hate the woman so much as he had, nor the doctor either. The bitterness went out of his face, and the sun was bright again. He got into the skiff and poled up the bayou and around the edges of the swamp. He tried to forget that the doctor had said Ma might die, and when he thought of the words, his face drew tight, and the hatred came back. He wished there was no such thing as sickness, so people like the doctor and the woman would never come to the swamp and to their house. When his mind was eased, he poled the skiff back to the house.

Theresa fixed dinner, but none of them ate very much. When they finished, Pa went in and woke the woman, and she went back to the room with Ma. Skeeter started in to see Ma, and the woman stopped him. She told him he couldn't come in and for none of them to ever come in the room until she said they could. The hatred returned to his face. Why should this woman tell him he could not go in the room to see his own mother? Why should she take away a privilege that he had known all his life? She was an outsider; she was not one of the family, so she had no right to do such a thing. He returned to the swamp and didn't come back until dark.

Pa and Skeeter ran the traps and line the next morning, and life returned to its usual path except for the woman's presence among them every day. She still would not allow them to enter the room, and the dark cloud of gloom hovered over the family. The food did not taste good, the river was not beautiful, and the joy of being alive had gone out of them. Things would be better if this woman would leave.

She stayed with them for two weeks, and then Pa took her back to town. She gave him several bottles of medicine to take back with instructions as to how to use them, and when Pa paid her for her services and the medicine, there was not a cent of the savings left. His chances for staying home during the summer were gone, but he didn't mind as long as Ma was going to live. When he returned home they all went in to see her for the first time. She was no longer fat, and her face was very pale. Her eyes were weak and drawn, but she gave them a faint smile. Skeeter left the room as soon as he could, for he didn't like to see his mother looking like this.

Theresa did the cooking and looked after Ma, while Pa and Skeeter carried on their work as usual. In a few days Ma could walk around a little with help, and she was gradually getting her strength back. The spring days vanished, and the hot summer came. The river was dropping, but the fishing was still good, even though they all knew that it wouldn't remain that way for long.

NINETEEN

FOR SOME STRANGE REASON the river didn't drop very fast that summer, and they still caught enough fish to keep them in supplies and save a small amount each week. By the middle of summer Ma was up and around again, though she would sometimes get weak and have to rest. She weighed much less than she had, and her face was still slightly drawn, but it would not be long until she was as well as she had ever been. The joy of living had returned to the family, and they were happy during the long hot days.

Skeeter was the happiest one of the family, for this was the time of year he loved most. He could go into the swamp at night to gig frogs, he could swim naked in the bayou, and he could drift in the skiff and let the hot sun tan his body as he watched the clouds roll by. Nothing was so wonderful as summer on the river, with the hot sun during the day and the big moon at night, and all the things he loved around him. He wished it would be summer the whole year.

The Hookers had been down to see Ma while the nurse was in the house, and they had not been able to see her. Pa and Skeeter were sitting on the porch one afternoon when they saw one of the Hooker boats coming up the bayou. The old man and woman and four of the boys were in it. Sparky was one of them. Pa and Skeeter went down to the landing to meet them.

"Howdy, Abner," said the old man. "Has that old woman left so'es we kin see Glesa yit?"

"She's been gone a good whiles now," said Pa. "Ma's been up and aroun' the house a lot lately. You folks git out and come on in the house."

They got out of the boat and went to the house as Theresa came to join Sparky. Skeeter stayed at the landing to be with the other three boys. The old people went to the front porch and sat down.

"We shore air glad to see you up and aroun' agin," said the old woman. "You give us a scare here fer a while."

"Hit give me a scare too," said Ma. "I could see them pearly gates openin' up fer a while. I shore thought I was gone, but I guess hit jest warn't my time yit."

"Well, I'm shore glad hit warn't yore time," said the old man. "We would have shore missed you if'n you had left."

"I think hit done her a little good," laughed Pa. "She's done lost all that weight, and now she looks to be a good twenty years younger."

"Well, derned if'n she don't at that," said the old man.

"You all jest teasin' me to make me feel good," said Ma. "You know I looks like a old scarecrow now."

"Well, if'n I thought hit would make me look twenty years younger, I'd git me a good case of the fever," said the old woman. "But you knows we jest teasin' you. You's lucky to be here now, cause don't many people git over the fever at all."

"I guess you air right," said Ma. "I'm jest plain lucky hit didn't git me."

"They's somethin' else we wanted to ask you folks abouts whiles we air neighborin'," said the old man. "Has you two ever decided ary thing yit about them two kids gittin' married? That boy of ourn air goin' to droop hisself to death if'n he don't find out somethin' soon. He droops aroun' like a sick cow ever' day, and spends most of his time messin' aroun' down by that big cypress tree."

"I think Theresa air jest about the same way," said Ma. "I don't think I ever seed two kids what had hit no worse."

"I been studyin' on that some myself," said Pa. "I thinks we ought to go on and sot a date so'es they kin know somethin'. Hit ain't fair to them if'n we don't. Whut do you all think would be a good time?"

"I don't rightly know," said the old man. "Some folks goes by the moon, and some folks the seasons, but I think one time air jest as good as another. I don't hold by them old ways no more. I think gittin' married air jest as good any time you wants hit."

"I likes Christmas mighty well," said the old woman.

"I think that's a powerful good idea too," said Ma. "We could git 'em married on Christmas Eve and then go down to the frolic at Mill Town that night to celebrate."

"I think that's the best," said the old man. "We'll jest call hit settled right here and now. They's goin' to git hitched Christmas Eve."

"I got to git the cloth purty soon to start makin' her a weddin' dress," said Pa. "Ain't no gal of ourn goin' to git married in nothin' less than the best."

"That shore air right," said Ma. "Hit'll take a long time to make that dress. You better git the cloth Satterday."

"I done got enough money put back to build them a house of their own right at the foot of that big cypress tree," said the old man. "And if'n they don't git busy right away and get me some little 'uns to play with, I'm goin' to move down there myself."

"Now you shet up talkin' like that," said the old woman. "You'll have the Coreys thinkin' you ain't got a brain left in you."

They all laughed and were in a good mood now that the plans had been completed for the wedding date.

"Who we goin' to git to do the marryin'?" asked Ma.

"We kin bring one of the preachers up from Mill Town that morning and take him back with us when we go down for the frolic that night," said Pa. "He kin be here fer the feast at dinner and git his bellyful fer a change."

"And I kin give him a snort of the best whiskey on Pearl River," said the old man. "That is, if'n he wants hit."

"Well, I don't speck he will," said the old woman.

"Why don't we call them kids in here and tell them the news and watch whut happens to their faces," said the old man.

"That would be a good idea," said Pa. "I'll go call 'em, and don't nobody let on likes they know whut hit is when they first gits here, and then we'll jest ups and tell 'em."

Pa went to the back stoop and called Sparky and Theresa and then hurried back to the front porch and sat down. In a few minutes they walked onto the porch and stood in front of the old people.

"Hit's a mouty purty day, ain't it?" said the old man.

"Hit shore air," said Theresa.

Sparky put his hands behind him and played with his fingers. They just stood there for a few minutes feeling awkward.

"We done decided to git you two married Christmas Eve," said the old man.

Sparky and Theresa turned and looked at each other for a few seconds without saying anything. Then he took her in his arms and kissed her for a long time. The old man jumped up and let out the loudest yell that had ever been heard on the Corey bayou. He jumped up and down and stomped his feet on the floor. Sparky and Theresa turned and ran from the porch.

"Sit down afore you stomps the house down!" shouted the old woman. "You gonna have the Coreys thinkin' you ain't got a speck of brains in you."

"I knowed that boy had it in him!" shouted the old man. "He's the only one that really takes after his Pa. I could do that back in my young days jest like he done it. I shore am proud of him."

"You jest carryin' on like a old fool," said the old woman. "Now sit down here afore you bust a blood vessel and falls out on the floor."

"Seein' somethin' like that makes me feel like a young buck again," said the old man. "I could go out right now and whup the biggest bear in them woods."

The kiss Sparky had given Theresa had affected all of them just as much as it had the old man, even though they didn't show it. The sight of such young love had thrilled them and warmed their old hearts.

"We better git on back to the house," said the old woman. "Hit's goin' to be dark afore long."

"I guess we had," said the old man. "I don't recall when I ever enjoyed a afternoon better, and I hates to leave."

When they got up and went down to the landing, Pa and Ma went with them. As Sparky left Theresa, he kissed her again, and the old man stood up in the boat and fired his gun into the air. He was still waving when the boat reached the mouth of the bayou and turned up the river. Theresa walked back to the house as if in a dream.

"Whut was all that about?" asked Skeeter.

"Sparky and Theresa air goin' to git married Christmas," said Pa.

"Aw, I thought hit were somethin'," said Skeeter.

*   *   *

When they were in town that Saturday, Pa went to buy the cloth for the dress while Skeeter went to see Uncle Jobe. Skeeter walked into the house and sat down.

"Howdy, Uncle Jobe," said Skeeter. "How you gittin' along now?"

"Old Uncle Jobe ain't fittin' fer nothin'," he said. "I ain't long fer this world, Massah Skeeter."

"You sick or somethin'?" asked Skeeter.

"I done been pegged, Massah Skeeter," he said. "They were a mean nigger come down here from the hills to work in the mill, and he were all time gittin' drunk and beatin' up folks, so nobody didn't like him, and he couldn't find no place to stay. He come here and asked me could he stay here, but I were afraid of him, so I told him no. He got mad and told me he were goin' to peg me. Ever time I done my job after that I kevered hit up so'es he couldn't find hit, but one day I done plumb forgot and didn't do hit. When I thought about hit, I went back to hide it, and afore I got there he had hit in a sack and were runnin' away, and now he done got me pegged."

"Whut you mean he done got you pegged?" asked Skeeter.

"When you pegs a feller, you bore a hole in a tree and then makes a peg to fit the hole. Then you take some uv his droppin's and puts in the hole, and everyday you knocks the peg in a little bit more. Ever time he hits that peg my body tightens up a little more, and the day that peg air knocked all the way in, my bowels air goin' to lock, and I's goin' to die a horrible death. Wouldn't nobody do sech a thing 'less he were in with the devil."

"Ain't they nothin' you kin do?" asked Skeeter. "Why don't you jest find the tree and pull the peg out?"

"Lawsy me, Massah Skeeter, I done looked at ever tree around here and ain't seed no sign uv hit."

"Can't you see the doctor and git some medicine fer it?"

"Hit ain't no use. They ain't nothin' you kin do once you air pegged but make yore peace with the Lord, and I's done that."

"I'll make Pa come early next Satterday and stay all day, and me and him'll shore find that peg fer you."

"I'd shore be mouty proud if'n you did."

"Well, don't you worry none. We'll git hit fer you fer shore."

Skeeter got up to leave, and the old Negro stopped him.

"Jest a minute afore you leaves, Massah Skeeter. Let this ole nigger give you a piece uv advice. I's done been here a long time, and these old eyes has seed a lot. I kin see things most folks can't, and I knows whut's goin' on along dis river. Dey's too much bad, and things ain't goin' right. De Lord ain't goin' to stand fer sech stuff much longer, people hatin' people and treatin' you river folks like skum. Tell yore pa to always stay as good a man as he is, and you do the same thing, Massah Skeeter. If things don't change, someday one of dem floods air goin' to fix dis river fer sho', and dem boats ain't goin' to be able to go up it, and you folks air goin' to have hit all to yoreself. Then you gwin know happiness."

"I'll tell him whut you said," said Skeeter, "and you take care of yoreself till we gits back next Satterday and helps you."

As Skeeter walked back up the lane to town, he had a funny feeling in his head. He didn't know what to think of the things Uncle Jobe had said for he had never heard talk like that before. He met Pa, and they made the trip back home in silence. Pa thought Skeeter looked strange, but he did not question him.

That night after supper the family was sitting on the porch, and Skeeter told them all about what Uncle Jobe had told him. He also gave Pa the message Uncle Jobe had sent to him.

"Them niggers with their hoodoo!" said Pa. "Hit beats ary thing I ever heard of. Tain't no use to worry 'bout him; he'll be all right."

"Whut if'n he ain't all right?" asked Skeeter.

"We'll go to town early next Satterday and make him take a good dose of medicine," said Pa, "and then we'll go out and find him a peg jest to make him feel good about hit. They ain't nothin' to that hoodoo, and hit couldn't possibly kill him."

"Whut about all that stuff he said 'bout the Lord goin' to do somethin' to the river?" asked Skeeter.

"That ain't nothin' to worry about, neither," said Pa. "Whut the Lord's goin' to do to a feller He's goin' to do anyway, so they ain't no use to try to run away from hit."

Skeeter thought about Uncle Jobe all the next week and kept wondering if the "hoodoo" was really true or not. He didn't believe it, but he couldn't forget the look of fear in the old Negro's eyes. It seemed to him that when Uncle Jobe talked of what the Lord was going to do he was looking right through him and into another world that he couldn't see. He would be glad when Saturday came and they could go back and see about him, but the days dragged by, and he thought the week would never end.

When the day did come, Skeeter could hardly wait until they reached the docks. He rowed the boat with all his strength, and several times Pa had to make him slow down. When the boat was tied, they took the fish to the market, and Skeeter started to leave.

"I'll be down there jest as soon as the fish air weighed and I gits the money," said Pa. "If'n he ain't all right, I'll come back up here and git the medicine."

Skeeter raced down the lane to the shack, and when he arrived Uncle Jobe was not sitting on the porch. He walked across the yard and sat down to wait. He thought Uncle Jobe should not have left, for he had told him they would be here early in the morning. A little Negro boy walked down the lane and stopped in front of the shack.

"You waitin' fer Uncle Jobe?" he asked.

"I shore am," said Skeeter. "You know where he's at?"

"Yassah," he said, "I knows where he's at."

"Then why don't you tell me," said Skeeter, "so'es I kin go meet him."

"He's daid. He died two days ago."

The thought didn't reach Skeeter at once, and he just sat and stared for a few minutes. Then he turned to the little Negro again.

"Where'd you say he was?"

"He's daid," repeated the little Negro.

This time the thought went through to Skeeter, and he fell to the floor and started crying bitterly. The little Negro moved away when he saw this. He lay on the floor and cried until he could not see. He was not aware that Pa was standing over him, and it startled him when Pa touched his shoulder. Pa did not have to ask what was wrong; he knew when he saw Skeeter lying there. He lifted Skeeter up, put his arms around his shoulders, and they started back to town. He did not try to stop Skeeter from crying, for he thought it would be best to let him stop when he wanted to.

He took Skeeter down to the boat and went back to town to buy the supplies. When he returned, Skeeter was still crying so he didn't bother him. He rowed the boat by himself and said nothing. When they were halfway home, Skeeter stopped crying and looked up at Pa.

"Why?" he asked.

"Hit's somethin' I can't explain to you, Son," said Pa. "When the Lord gits ready fer a person, he jest takes him back up where he come from, and they ain't nothin' we kin do about hit. Ole Uncle Jobe were mighty old, and he had seed his life, so hit were time fer him to go. He'll be a heap better off where he air now, and I know he wouldn't want to see you carry on so. You ought to be proud fer him, cause he's at a good place, and he's where he's been wantin' to be. They ain't nothin' but happiness there, and hit's all spring and summer. The rations is always good, and ole Uncle Jobe will like hit mighty fine."

Skeeter stopped crying and lay down in the bottom of the boat. Presently he leaned over the side and washed his face in the muddy water and then took his oar from Pa. When they got home, Skeeter went straight to his room and went to bed without eating supper. Ma started to call him, but Pa told her to leave him alone. He told her about Uncle Jobe being dead, and she understood.

The next morning Skeeter ate a light breakfast and left in the skiff. He wanted to go to the swamp for there was something about it that took the sadness and hatred from him. It gave him a feeling that nothing else could give him. He stayed there all day, and it was dark when he got back to the landing. The sadness was gone from him, and he was glad that Uncle Jobe would be happy. He walked into the kitchen and the family was all waiting there.

"I'm powerful hungry," he said, "and as soon as the supper air done I'm goin' in the swamp and gig us some frogs. Them legs shore would be good fer breakfast in the mornin'."